The Sign of the Scorpion

An Erotic Mystery Story

J. Gonzo Smith

Blue Moon Books, Inc.
New York

Sign of the Scorpion
ISBN 1-56201-094-8
CIP data available from the Library of Congress

Manufactured in the United States of America
Published by Blue Moon Books, Inc.
61 Fourth Avenue
New York, NY 10003

Cover design by Steve Brower

Chapter 1

"*There's* a young lady here who wants to see you, sir," said Jackson. "She says she's a cousin of yours, but." The inter-office receiver buzzed for a thoughtful second, and the distorted metallic voice broke through the hum to add, "She says she's your cousin Clara. ."

"Blonde?" the District Attorney asked doubtfully

"Brunette!" Jackson was triumphantly certain that he had now intercepted an impostor, possibly one with a bottle of acid or a snub-nosed automatic in her purse

"Oh, my brunette cousin Clara! Send her in!"

She was eighteen, and it was still a novelty to her to have a man rise politely when she came into a room The door was quite a way from the desk, and again she was aware of her body's swing, that hint of her immaturity which she was always trying to disguise

"I'm sorry to intrude in this way, Mr. Garnett," she said to the D.A. apologetically, but with a proud note in her voice. "I just had to see you somehow though. . ."

"Yes, of course." He felt the chill of her fingers and smiled pleasantly at her. "Please sit down." He made her feel that she had been standing there for several ungraceful and tedious minutes. "I always see people who use the slightest ingenuity in getting past that secretary of mine . . . but that cousin touch is pretty lame, you know. Next time think of something a little better."

She smiled faintly. "My name is Clara Reeves," she told him. "I don't think I'm anybody's cousin. So far as I know my sister is my only relative. My parents are dead, and . . ." She was blushing slightly, and that pleased him.

He let his eyes wander from hers and follow the outlines of her face. A soft oval, and very attractive. She could have done her hair in a more becoming manner, but the dark curls were well suited to a young girl. Hair so very black was quite unusual with blue eyes, he thought. She had smudged the lipstick on her full mouth. Her girlish breasts were maturing, as could be seen from the way the nipples thrust themselves tautly against the white satin of her blouse.

"Well, what's your trouble, Miss Reeves?" he said, in a voice as matter of fact as he could make it.

She leaned forward in the deep leather chair, and the frown of worry deepened on her brow. "It's Rita, my elder sister. She . . . she's disappeared!" She paused after this brief announcement, as if she expected him to produce her sister from his coat pocket. As her revelation had no result whatever, beyond a professionally noncommittal nod, she added, "She's been gone over a week already."

"How soon did you go to the police?" he asked, when no more information seemed to be forthcoming. "What are they doing about it?"

She looked startled. "I haven't been to the police," she said in a low voice. "They'd only ask a couple of questions and then add her name to a list of dozens of other missing persons. And I want to see something done about it. I really want to find her."

"But my dear Miss Reeves . . . what in the world do you want me to do about it? I'm only a District Attorney. The Bureau of Missing Persons was created specifically to trace people who suddenly drop out of sight. My job is to deal with criminals." He saw the tears waiting to fall, and hurried to change his tactics. "But if there is something really wrong, maybe you'd better tell me."

She lifted her face to his. "I'm afraid it is a criminal case," she said. "That's the whole thing."

"Well then, tell me all about it. Tell me something about yourself too, your background . . . all there is to tell. That may be very important." He looked at her questioningly.

"I have only one sister . . . or had," Clara began. "Her name is Rita. She's twenty and very lovely." For a moment she looked as if she would cry, but she pulled herself together and went on. "We've been living alone together ever since our aunt died three years ago. I realize now that Rita was keeping some things from me . . . and that's not a bit like her. We never had any secrets from each other before, until she began spending weekends away from home. Long weekends too, from Friday to Tuesday. I never saw any of the people she went with, either.

"She used to drive off in her roadster, and she'd come back alone. And when I asked if I could go with her she only laughed and kissed me and told me not to be a little silly." Clara shook her head at her own thoughts. "Last Friday she told me she was going to spend the weekend in the country, she didn't say where. She never came back on Tuesday or on the next day either, but I got a long distance call from her that day saying she wouldn't be back till Thursday. She was so vague and strange about it, and then she never came back after all, and here it is Monday again, and I'm so terribly worried I don't know what to do about it all."

"I still don't see it's anything I can interfere in," said the D.A. as he leaned back in his chair. "Unless you really believe that she's been mixed up in something criminal, and I don't see anything to give you that idea."

"I haven't told you everything yet," Clara replied. "You see, when I really began to worry about her . . . that was on the Friday . . . I had the idea that I'd try and find out something about the parties and weekends she'd been going on. So I went through her things. And I found something awfully peculiar in them. So I'm afraid Rita really has been kidnaped . . . or even worse."

Garnett turned his head to study the girl's face. "Why do you believe that?" he asked quietly.

Strangely enough, the question made the girl blush furiously. She lowered her eyes, looked up at him again, but could not meet his steady gaze. When she answered she looked down fixedly at her gloved hands.

"I know it was wrong to go through Rita's things," she said, "but I love her so much and I was only trying to protect her. I know she was the elder, but still I was so worried about her. So I pried open a drawer she always kept locked, and in there I found the most unbelievable kinds of things. There were funny kinds

6

of books, and all sorts of things I'd rather not talk about, if you don't mind. And Rita's diary was there too. It was terrible, some of the things she had written there. Someone . . . someone quite horrible . . . was influencing my sister, and her diary showed what an awful thing that influence was. It's filled with stories of some gang of people she'd been mixed up with, and what she'd seen them do. And then I found this. . . ."

From her purse the girl took a large silver ring and gave it to Conrad. It held an enormous onyx, into the polished face of which, in gold, an exquisitely chased figure had been set.

"A scorpion," he said, balancing the ring in his palm. "It's beautiful workmanship." He turned it around and examined it more closely, holding it to the light.

"A man's ring," Clara added. "Rita never showed it to me. But I'm sure it had something to do with her disappearance. That isn't just a ring . . . it's a symbol of something evil. And if that isn't enough . . . I found a bookplate with the same design pasted in all those dreadful books in her drawer."

"But you haven't told me what the books were," Conrad said inquiringly.

Clara blushed scarlet. "You'd have to see them for yourself to understand," she said, her eyes averted. "I just could not describe them to you . . . I'd die of shame. But if you could come over this evening. . . ." She gave him a card with her address in a tiny back-hand script.

"I'll be glad to," he said, as he slipped the card into his pocket. "And for the present would you like to leave the ring with me for safekeeping?"

7

"Oh, yes!" said Clara, looking at the ring with distaste. "I don't want it. And thank you very much, Mr. Garnett. . . ."

"Not at all," he assured her. "And I'll be around about eight tonight and we'll look into all this. In the meantime don't worry too much about your sister. I'm pretty sure no harm has come to her. And in the meantime . . . better not mention our discussion to anyone else. We never know who may be concerned, until we find out more details." He smiled at her, willing her to smile back, and she did.

"Thank you so much," she said again as she rose. And he watched her walk toward the door, allowing himself time to admire her graceful figure before going forward to open the door for her. He noticed the curve of her hips and the pressure of her skirt on her buttocks, and it was not hard to picture her walking naked. And he wondered what she was wearing under the cool summer suit, and he imagined a pair of sheer silk pants caught in the cleft of her soft thighs, the pink flesh showing through, with a light edging of lace lending charm to the whole ensemble.

He saw her to the outer office, and she turned once more to smile at him as she left. His lips moved in a final "good-bye." But she was too far away to know it, or to guess that the words his lips actually said were, "You'll be a lovely creature to fuck, darling!"

"Jackson," he said aloud, when the girl had left, "did you know I had a criminal mind? Set a thief to catch a thief, you know." And he turned back into his office and closed the door.

Chapter 2

She came toward him as though she were going to kiss him, and he involuntarily reached his arms toward her. But she merely took his hat and put it away. He followed her into the living room, jealous of the light summer dress which clung so possessively to her girlish body.

"Will you have a gin rickey?" she asked. "It's so warm this evening."

"Yes, thanks," he smiled. "Can I help?"

"You can squeeze the lemons, if you want," she said.

Standing beside her as they mixed the drinks, he was by now already intoxicated with the scent that her movements were bringing him . . . the heady mixture of youthful sweat and good soap, delicate perfume, and clean cunt. His glance dropped to her girlish breasts, his mind already between her thighs.

"No news from your sister?" he asked.

"Nothing at all," said Clara gloomily.

"Now don't be so gloomy about it. I promise you we'll find her somehow." And he patted her arm reassuringly.

"Let's take our drinks out on the terrace. It's cooler out there," she suggested.

"You have a larger place here than I had imagined," he said, as they sat looking out across the garden. He toyed with his glass and watched her through half-closed eyes as she leaned back in her chair. A breeze rustled through the dusk and toyed with her dress, promising to play interesting tricks there if he would be patient.

"This was my parents' house," Clara said, as she sipped her drink. "That's really why we live here. I'd much rather live in the city. It's so dull here." She shifted restlessly as she spoke.

"I imagine so," replied Conrad. The breeze had lifted up her skirt just as Clara uncrossed her legs. Unnoticed by her in the gathering darkness, her dress now lay across her thighs, above the rolled stockings. Her knees, dimpled and smooth, seemed to smile at the District Attorney. He gulped his drink, and appreciated as much of the view as he could, pitting his eyesight against the dusk. Had Clara's legs been covered by her dress, nothing unusual would have been disclosed by her posture. But with her limbs bare where her skirt had gently fallen back, she seemed to have taken a particularly suggestive pose. Her knees were turned slightly outward, and the naked inner sides of her thighs thus in sight made it appear that rather more was being displayed than was actually the case.

Conrad made some vague remark. While he was speaking she drew one knee up. He finished his sentence, still looking into her eyes, and nothing in his manner indicated that he had seen or noticed anything out of the ordinary. But the whole underside of her slender leg, the side toward him, was offered to his view from knee to buttock. Her skin was pink under its coating of tan, and he could even see the line of lighter color where her bathing suit had protected her during the sunny days. Where the naked leg joined its twin on the seat there was . . . there was . . . no, it was growing dark and there was nothing. He sighed, but his disappointment did not sour him to the point of turning his eyes elsewhere. He continued to make light conversation while enjoying the effects of the gin and also the full pleasure of the flesh. He drank slowly so as not to push Clara into getting up to mix him another.

She wanted to talk about her sister Rita, and relate little stories of their childhood and their parents' death. But when the friendly breeze grew spiteful and swished her skirt downward across her legs again, Conrad became tired of the terrace and rose to his feet.

She jumped up from her chair. "We'll go in," she said, "and I'll show you what I found." And inside the house she turned to him and asked, "Shall I bring the drawer down or would you rather see it where I found it? That might be best if you don t mind. It's in her bedroom upstairs."

He followed her up the stairs, stifling the sudden urge to put his hand in between the legs that moved so enticingly just ahead of him, and see if her cunt was as he had imagined it. But it would startle her, he realized, and she would very probably be bone-dry there anyway. So he followed her into her sister's bedroom without a word. Clara unlocked a bureau drawer with a nail file, her expert touch showing that she had been to that drawer before, particularly since she discovered its contents.

11

"I could put the drawer on the bed if you want to look at it," she said. So they sat on the bed with the drawer between them.

"First of all," he said, "we have. . ."

"Oh! Those are mine!" Clara exclaimed, snatching from his hand a pair of light green silk panties which lay on top of a thick morocco-bound book. She hustled the panties out of sight and moved closer to him. He was examining the pictures with which the black book was embellished

"I thought that was Rita's drawer?" Conrad suggested.

"Oh! I was using those old silk things to dust with the day I discovered this," Clara explained lamely. She was rosy with blushes, and Conrad eyed her with some amusement. He could almost see her wondering whether it was true that hair grows on your palm if you play with yourself, and then everybody can see it and guess that. . . . But he was noncommittal.

"That's it. Yes, a dustcloth. I see." He returned to his inspection of the drawer and its contents, laying them out on the bed as he did so. He put down the black book and picked up a smaller one in padded leather with a miniature lock which did not lock. It was Rita's diary obviously. The handwriting was soft and slanting. Then there was an envelope of silk with Chinese characters on it in red brush strokes. Contents . . . Clara averted her eyes . . . six condoms of fine manufacture and curiously armed with an array of rubber fins, spikes, knobs, whiskers, etc. Next . . . a book of etchings, hand tinted in water colors, and a scorpion bookplate in the front. A glance was sufficient to explain the type of etchings that these were. The D.A.'s eyes lingered for a moment on a picture of two girls sixty-nining as they swung through the air, supported by flying rings in which the one who had hehead downward had hooked her knees. Clara could not help peeking to see what had attracted his attention. He looked up suddenly, and she blushed and then swallowed hard.

Next came a small case of shantung silk with an ivory clasp. Inside were two silver balls somewhat smaller than a walnut. They rang gaily when Conrad shook them gently. Clara looked puzzled, and he knew she was too shy to ask for an explanation.

"Japanese," he said. "Rinnotama set." Clara nodded as if she really knew what he was talking about. Then came three small volumes, each with the now familiar scorpion bookplate in it: "Memoirs of Casanova," "Sixty-nine Delightful Ways to Sin," "The Art of the Tongue," and "Ten Inches Above the Garter." The last two were bound in one volume, illustrated with many photographs. After this came an object which was and yet was not a male organ. It was a rubber replica, lifelike in its proportions and design, hollow and therefore springy to the touch, and made to fit standards in size which any woman would admit were exacting, to say the least of it. Clara's cheeks were crimson as she looked away while Conrad examined it, and then laid it also on the bed.

Finally, there was a cat-of-nine-tails, but with only five tails. It was of the finest and softest leather, wound and braided with the utmost care, and Conrad wondered just what stories of amorous conflict it could disclose if it were not mute. They sat there in the midst of Rita's secret sex life, like two castaways on a raft, and for a long time neither of them spoke. At last, in desperation, Clara broke the silence. "What do you make of it?" she asked.

"It's very interesting," said Conrad, "very interesting indeed. But I don't know that it helps us much. Unless the diary . . . you've read it, haven't you?" Clara blushed and nodded. He picked it up and riffled through the pages, finally selecting one and then knitting his brow over it. "I don't seem to be able to read your sister's handwriting," he said as he handed it to Clara. "Would you mind reading me these two or three pages?"

"Oh! But really!" Clara protested. "Why! The words are so dreadful . . . I really couldn't."

"Come now, don't be silly!" he said firmly. "How else are we to investigate this affair?" He moved aside some of the objects on the bed and sat next to her. "Now then, begin with this entry," he said, pointing.

"It was wonderful last night," began Clara in a low voice and after a moment's hesitation. "It was more wonderful than ever, just as it always seems to be." She stopped uncertainly.

"Fine," he encouraged her, "that's very good. I couldn't make out a word of it myself."

"I went up to his apartment and he was waiting for me," Clara recommenced, her voice more determined but still a little shaky. "We didn't say a word, but he kissed me as soon as I was inside the door. When he did that our bodies clung together, and I knew that he had been thinking about me for I felt . . . I felt. . . ."

"Go on," said Conrad, "what's the matter?"

'But I can't read that word!" exclaimed Clara, blushing.

He took the book from her hands and pretended to study it for a moment. "Prick," he said, "felt his prick. She says she felt his prick. Go on." He gave the book back to her.

"But I can't read words like that out loud to you!" Clara protested. She was blushing crimson as she spoke, and at the same time asking herself why Conrad was persuading her to do this She refused to accept the reason that came to her mind at that moment. Really, Conrad was terrible, she told herself.

He took Clara's hand. "My dear girl," he said, "I'm sorry to have to ask you to do this. But I'm the only one who hears you say them, and I know it's not you but Rita who is speaking. You must do it if we are to learn what has happened to her. Every word in this diary may be important to us."

"I'll try," Clara whispered in a low voice, and Conrad patted her knee. "Good girl," he said.

Clara read on. "I knew that he had been thinking about me for I felt his . . . prick pressing against my body. We simply ran into the living room, and there . . . in front of his Chinese idol . . . I took off my things. I shook the snow from my coat and then I stripped from head to foot, without pausing My darling simply stood and stared while I threw off my clothes, for I was in a perfect fury to be rid of them and have him on me instead. But still I remembered how he liked to see me in progressive stages of undress, and I took just enough time to let him appreciate every individual charm as it appeared. I looked back at him over my shoulder as I took off my snow boots, after my dress and coat and undies were gone, and how his eyes glowed with desire. I knew he could see my pussy between the cheeks of my bottom, and that it excited him terribly. Men are really so silly.

"Just as soon as I was stark naked I ran to the fire, which was just burning up nicely, and stood by it pretending to warm my behind. I wasn't altogether pretending either, for it was terribly cold outside. Then he came across the room and said that he would warm my backside for me, so I brought over a footstool and bent my bare body across it so that he could switch my bottom good and hard. You can imagine how that warmed both of us. Then when he saw I was smarting beautifully he tossed the switch into the fire and began to undress.

"I lay at his feet watching him while he took off his clothes. My backside was burning and my slit itched like fire. A spanking is certainly one of the ways to begin to make love. And it's wonderful to belong so completely to a man that you even like him to beat you! As soon as he was naked I pulled myself to my knees and began to kiss his thighs and sex. But he wouldn't let me take it in my mouth just then, no matter how much I begged him. We lay on the sofa for a while side by side, while he teased me with his cock. I thought he would never let me have it, but at last he allowed me to hold it in my hand and play with it, and as soon as I was clasping it warmly between my legs against the hair of my pussy it got simply enor-

16

mous, and then in a little while he began to squeeze the tip inside my yielding slit. . . .

"You can imagine I was anything but cold now, but I was shivering with passion . . . and he teased me, asking me if I wanted another switching. Stupidly joking, I said, 'Yes, as long as I get something else with it,' never imagining that he'd take me seriously.

"But he fetched another switch, and this time made me lie full length on the sofa with my face buried in the pillows so that he could whip the whole of my naked body. This second spanking was much harder than the first, and the tears really came. But I wouldn't have stopped him for the world. I could see his prick just rampant, every time I turned my head on the pillows, and the tears in my eyes seemed to drive him wild. Finally my thighs and bottom were red all over and burned like fire. I was on fire inside too, and I could hardly wait for him to mount me.

"I rolled over on my back and opened my legs to him . . . gripping his thighs and groaning as my sore buttocks rubbed against the cushions. I was so excited that my thighs and the sofa underneath were simply flooded, and the lips of my slit were open and disclosed all my most secret charms. He threw himself on top of me in a fury of desire, and I felt his prick thrusting down between my parted thighs. All my ardent body pressed upward to welcome him in an unconscious gesture of passion, and I gasped out sentences of amorous longing as we clung together.

" 'Ahh! Ahh!' I exclaimed. 'Here I am all naked in your arms! You are the first man to see me all naked

17

like this! Do you really want me? Feel how much I want you! I'm simply overflooding there already! Quick! Quick! Touch me there! No! No, higher up! It's maddening to be touched there by a man! Go on! Go on! Oh! Oh! Your prick is hurting me! It's too big! You can't get it in! Oh! Oh! You must! You must! Wait till I open my legs wider! That's better! Now kiss my breasts! Oh! Ohhh! Don't bite them! Did you ever take a girl like this before? It's so exciting! I never thought it would be like this! Ohh! Ohh! You can't get it any further! Yes! You can! You must! I want you so! Push! Push! Now it's coming! Ahh! Ahh! Now I can feel you all the way up inside me! Quick! Quick! I'm coming! Can you come too? Don't stop! Don't stop! Take me! Take me! Now! Now! Oh! Ohh! Ohhhh!'

"I lay back exhausted and broken as he slipped out of me, and the whole room seemed to swing around in giddy circles. I felt that I loved him with all my body and soul. In my passion I was clutching his balls so roughly that I must have hurt him with my nails. But neither of us cared just then. And after a little while I reached down and began to caress his limp sex to see whether I could get a hard on it once more, so that he would want me again. But he said I was too keen, and told me to pick up my clothes and come upstairs to bed."

"Let's not bother with that upstairs part just now," Conrad suggested. "Why, Clara darling, you're trembling all over. What's the matter?" He reached out a hand and stroked the dark hair, drawing Clara gently toward him as he did so.

"I just can't believe it," she faltered weakly. "That

Rita, my own sister . . . that she'd . . . that she could do . . ." His shoulder was there to lean against, so Clara nestled to it. How silly it seemed that the flower in his lapel tickled her nose and made her want to sneeze, and not to cry the way she had been going to. His arm went around her. It was cozy and warm. Her breasts felt funny and their nipples ached. "I don't know what you must think of me?" she whispered softly into his coat collar.

"But why in the world? You haven't done any of these sort of things, have you?" he inquired.

"No! No, of course not! Why, I've never even thought of them before!" She looked up at him with dewy eyes. "You believe me, don't you? I never even heard of things like that till I found out what was in this drawer." She seemed begging to be reassured.

"But you do think about them now? Now that you have found out?" His eyes roamed to where he had watched her hide the silk panties, and her eyes followed his guiltily.

"I . . . I can't help thinking about them sometimes. And those books . . the dreadful things there are in those books. . . ." Clara faltered.

Conrad drew her gently down toward him. Together they settled back on the cushions, and Clara discovered with a dazed sort of recognition that she was lying side by side with the District Attorney on the bed. She would have thought more about it if she had not been busy noticing the way a few curls of gray hair showed at his temples. It was so distinguished, she thought vaguely. He was soothing and caressing her, and before she had realized it he was kissing her too, and her lips were parted by the tip of a searching, eager tongue. She was a little shocked at first, but something inspired her to touch the tip of his tongue with the tip of hers, timidly at first and then more and more responsively, as his kisses drew moist passion from her mouth. Her mind suddenly took control again, and she pulled away from him, her cheeks red with embarrassment. But he did not let her think about that for long.

"You know," he told her, patting her leg, "I have a plan that I think will lead to your sister, wherever she may be now. There's a bare chance, of course, that she may return on her own, but from what we read in that diary I imagine she likes her present situation well enough to stay with it. So we'll have to find her . . . you'll have to find her . . . I should say."

"What do I do? Tell me quickly what must I do?" inquired Clara, eagerly turning toward him with a most appealing look in her blue eyes.

"Well, if there is such a person as the scorpion ring seems to indicate, then he'll be pretty anxious not to have it lying about now that Rita has vanished. So tomorrow we'll put an 'ad' in the paper, saying that such a ring has been found. And if he shows up perhaps you can find out something about him personally, and also where he comes from."

"And find out where those terrible orgies take place that Rita mentions in her diary?" Clara cried.

"Yes . . . and also where she is now," Conrad amended. "But . . . you'll have to show plenty of nerve, Clara. And . . . well . . . he may take a fancy to you . . . like he did to Rita. . . ." Conrad paused expressively.

Clara blushed scarlet. "You mean I'd have to let . . . ?" Words failed her as she remembered the scenes from her sister's diary and realized the implication in the D.A.'s remarks. She faltered and then began again. "You really think . . . but how . . . he couldn't . . . I mean it isn't possible he'd . . . want to . . . try to." Poor Clara gave it up and put both hands over her hot cheeks.

"Yes, Clara, you would. He might want to make love to you. In fact, considering the type of man he is, he's almost certain to want to. You're so fresh and young and attractive. Why, a man would have to be made of stone to resist . . . and this Scorpion seems to be quite uninhibited. If you meet him, if he takes you somewhere in his car perhaps, he might want to kiss you, to hold you tightly in his arms like this. . . ."

"How awful!" exclaimed Clara, unconsciously responding with her warm young body to Conrad's embrace.

"He would probably caress your thighs too. Like this! And then he would kiss you again." Conrad kissed her until Clara went limp in his arms. He found her young breasts and pressed them ardently. His searching fingers trespassed beneath her dress and gently squeezed her nipples until they hardened under his touch. "He might even want to fuck you, Clara!" he said very softly.

"He wouldn't!" Clara was so violent in her outburst that she sat up and thrust Conrad's hands away from her.

"But if finding Rita depended on it?" he asked gently.

She bit her lip and tried to look resolute. "Well . . .

21

I love Rita so much. I suppose I'd do anything to find her and bring her back. But I've never done anything like that. I don't know if I could. I . . . I . . . well . . . yes, I would. To get Rita back. I'd let him do anything he wanted."

"I don't believe you could. I don't think you could even take off your clothes in front of a man without dying of shame. Could you undress in front of me right now?" Conrad demanded.

"But nothing depends on it now!" She hesitated for a moment.

"No! But when it does you won't be able to cope with the situation, I'm afraid. You're willing to help, but I don't much think you could go through with it. After all, you're a virgin and that . . ."

"I wouldn't be scared," Clara insisted. "Not if getting Rita back depended on it. I have plenty of nerve. . . ."

"Never enough to pretend that I'm this Scorpion person and that I've just told you I won't tell you where your sister is unless you strip to the skin this minute. That might be what would happen, you know, and with no more warning." The D.A. looked at her with a question in his eye.

"I have plenty of nerve. . . . I'll show you . . ." repeated Clara, as she rose to her feet. She was blushing and she was trembling also. The D.A. was trembling too, but not so visibly. It excited him to see her so overwrought.

"All right! I'll show you!" said Clara defiantly as she began to unfasten her dress. It was belted at the waist, and she released the buckle and tossed the belt onto a chair. Then she opened a zipper at the side and the white flesh of her youthful body showed temptingly between the edge of her bra and the top of her panties as her dress gaped open all the way down.

"Do you really mean me to undress?" she faltered, as if hoping for a reprieve. Conrad shrugged his shoulders as if to say "I told you that you hadn't the nerve," and Clara bit her lip and stooped to gather the folds of her skirt in both hands, raising it over her bare thighs to her hips and allowing him to admire the lacy panties that he had only imagined before. She wriggled a moment before she managed to slip the dress over her head, a slight tug being necessary to persuade it past the enchanting swell of her girlish breasts.

Her undies, what there was of them, fitted her like a dream. But even a dream seemed superfluous in concealing such a body. At his appreciative nod she unfastened her bra, but she did it the hard way, slipping the shoulder straps off first and then reaching behind her to undo the snap. By that time, of course, both pink nipples were peeping out, and as she released the elastic the whole bra fell away along her arms, revealing all her girlish bosom. Her swelling breasts were so youthful, with their tender curves and the shadowed groove between them, that Conrad could hardly restrain himself from kissing them forthwith.

But he realized that her school-girl modesty would very probably be alarmed if he made such a gesture while her own desires were still unawakened. "You have more nerve than I thought," he told her as she stood hesitantly before him.

Clara blushed deeply as she stooped to remove her

shoes, and her twin breasts swung down slowly and temptingly. Their pendent motion seemed to embarrass her, and she took off the other shoe by raising her foot up and to one side. This gesture lifted their swelling curves instead, and the D.A. longed to reach out and caress the pink tips until they hardened with desire. But once more he refrained. He must not alarm the quarry when it was almost within his reach. Possession of an inexperienced young girl was of course a thrill, but then the sensation of the chase was even more delightful. To lure a virgin into surrender when she was almost willing to be seduced and yet fought half-heartedly against it, this was a game which both instinct and intellect could enjoy.

With her shoes off Clara looked younger and more helpless than ever. And the gesture with which she rolled down her stockings and pulled them off was exciting, less because it revealed the curling sex-hair under the edge of her panties than because it made her handle her own naked thighs, and thus become aware that she was stripping herself naked before a man's eager eyes, and displaying to him all her most secret charms.

She leaned against a chair while she removed her silk stockings and tossed them onto its seat, and then . . . turning away from Conrad's gaze, she slipped down her panties in three quick movements, sliding her hands down her flanks and under the elastic at her waist, pushing the clinging silk over her hips and off her rounded thighs, and finally stepping out of the lacy circle that lay round her pink little feet. She did not even try to hide the diamond shaped patch of curling hair at her crotch which half-concealed her sex, although her hands fluttered downward as if she wanted to but had determined to be brave.

"You've never undressed in front of a man before, have you?" he asked softly.

"Oh! No, never!" she faltered. Her voice was low, and when he beckoned to her she went to him and sat down on the bed, hiding her face in her hands. "Have I nerve enough?" she asked him questioningly. But he did not answer her immediately, instead pushing her gently down beside him as he lay looking at her upturned face with its quivering lips, and softly but insistently caressing her body with his free hand. She did not say anything in response, but neither did she make any objection to his gentle overtures.

He stroked her with tender fingers from shoulder to knee, tickling her nipples, molding her lovely breasts, smoothing her soft stomach, and even probing gently between her closed thighs. She tried to cross her arms over her girlish breasts so as to protect their pink nipples, although she did not seem to mind about the delicate line of her sex which he could just discern at the juncture of her thighs. She really puzzled him.

"Why do you let me do this to you?" he asked her, passing his hand lightly across her belly.

"Because you told me to," she said. "You said you wanted to find out if I had enough nerve to meet the Scorpion, and I wanted to show you that I had, that's all." She blushed and bit her lip. "I'm so terribly ashamed," she added. "I wish you wouldn't look at me when you feel me, or feel me when you look at me. I feel so ashamed when you look at me and touch me at the same time."

"Are you sure you aren't letting me do this because you want me to?" asked Conrad, as his fingers plucked gently at the dark hair on her mount.

"No! Oh, no! I don't want you to do it at all! It makes me want to go away in a corner and cry. I hate it!" And poor Clara did look like tears just then.

"And do you hate me too?" queried the D.A. gently.

"No, I don't hate you. Men are like that, I guess. But I know I shouldn't let you do it, even for Rita's sake. I did not know you would want to do this to me when I asked you to come here tonight."

"Will you read some more of Rita's diary to me now?" Conrad asked. "Will you lie here naked, just as you are, and read to me?"

"If you say I have to, I will!" she answered, with her eyes tightly closed.

He gave her a book. It was not Rita's diary. "Read some of that to me," he said, and he moved closer, feeling her with his body as well as his hands.

"Why are you doing this to me?" she asked him as she opened the book. Whatever was in her voice, it was not exactly resentment. She was incredulous and she was ashamed, but she was not resentful. There was a passive forbearance in the way she accepted his actions which puzzled him. It was almost as if she were coming to display a little more than acceptance only, he thought.

"Because if you do find this Scorpion person," he said glibly, "you'll find yourself obliged to do things of which you have never even heard. If you're going to crack up I want to know it right now . . . before we make any further plans. If you break down somewhere else, and he finds out what you're up to, you might be in the gravest danger."

"I told you before that I could do anything that I had to do," Clara said. Her voice was low and trembled so much that he did not think she was able to read aloud, but she could and she did.

"I was only fourteen," the book began, "when my cousin Robert and his friend Henri gave me my first lesson in love, one which I have never forgotten. I was just going down to the garden to pick some cherries for dinner when Robert called to me from his room . . . 'Marie, will you come here for a moment.'

"Without the slightest suspicion I entered the room, and no sooner was I inside than I found myself seized from behind and Robert exclaimed, 'Shut the door quickly, Henri, and help me hold her!' And before I could enter a word of protest the two boys began to undress me.

"I had really no defense against them, for to have called out for help would only have made matters worse if someone had heard me and entered the room. So you can imagine what happened. In no time at all their eager hands had dragged my dress off over my head, and there I was, standing before them in my undies . . . and blushing scarlet with embarrassment. But even at such a moment I thought with satisfaction that they were my best silk undies, through which my girlish body would show to its best advantage.

"But this was only the beginning of things! Without

27

the least hesitation Robert released my shoulder straps and slipped my chemise down to my waist, while Henri stooped down and began to remove my shoes and stockings. I was so astonished by their audacity that I scarcely uttered a word when they unfastened my bra and revealed my naked little breasts.

"Then they pulled down my panties and there I stood, as naked as the day I was born, only a far more enticing picture now. My twin breasts with their pink nipples would have seduced a monk from virtue, while the curling hair which showed at the triangle of my slender thighs offered little protection to my deliciously tempting slit.

"What a time those youngsters had with me. Fastening my hands and ankles with their belts and ties, they bound me very securely to the four posts of the bed, with my slender arms and legs stretched to their fullest extent. In this helpless position I was forced to display all those secret charms which had hitherto been closely concealed, but which were now fated to endure their amorous assaults.

" 'See what tiny breasts she has,' said Robert, as he tickled my pink nipples, 'and look how the hair curls up from her mount and over her slit as if to hide it from us. But I'll soon alter that.' And with caressing fingers the youngster began to expose more fully the delicious secrets of my shadowed cleft. As he parted the folded lips of my virgin cunt his ardent touch discovered my clitoris, which hardened little by little under his eager examination until I was sighing with sensuous delight.

"After spending several minutes in thus teasing the

most sensitive parts of my girlish body, squeezing my tender breasts till the nipples hardened like two red cherries, and passing tantalizing fingers up and down my sex until it was all moist and throbbing with desire, they then proceeded to undress.

"I had never seen a man naked before, and blushingly turned away as they took off their last garments, but when Robert approached the bed I must admit I peeped at the weapon with which I expected him to attack me. But perhaps he realized that a girl takes longer than a man to become warmed up for love and for this reason delayed his intended seduction.

"Thus, instead of attempting to penetrate me **at** once, he knelt above my trembling body and thrust his penis into the valley between my breasts, where it left a trail which bore witness to its virile excitement. Then he demanded that I kiss its tip, and then caress it with my lips and tongue.

" 'How can you possibly ask such a thing, Robert?' I gasped, 'I can't . . . I simply can't kiss your . . . thing . . . like that. You know I can't.' And I began to cry.

" 'You'll do just as he says,' interrupted Henri, pinching my nipples with cruel fingers. And so despite my fear and shame I was forced to lift my face and kiss the red-tipped penis that confronted me. Then I parted my lips and let it slip into my mouth, where I felt sure its size alone would choke me.

"Bending down above me, Robert proceeded to finger my utterly defenseless slit, until I could feel its lips parting and becoming moist with desire. 'Now suck me with your lips while you tickle the tip with your tongue,' he said. 'You've no idea how exciting your mouth is when you do that. I shall come in a minute if you're not careful. . . . '

"It seemed as if I must yield or be choked by this huge cock, so I decided to obey his command. A decision which may sound strange and which seemed to me then to be horrible, but which I discovered later to be not altogether unpleasant. In fact I was learning the lesson of love much faster than might have been expected.

"So while Robert thrust his weapon to and fro in my warm mouth until the tip seemed to touch the back of my throat, Henri amused himself by lying across my naked body and rubbing his penis up and down the parted lips of my consentient slit.

"I was panting with excitement and desire by this time, and the room seemed to be going round and round. Henri had now thrust his cock up and down between my thighs until I was all wet inside and open to any attack, and when he realized this from an involuntary movement of my hips and mount he parted my legs still further and began to invade me in real earnest.

"My mouth was sore from Robert's furious thrusts, and my bruised thighs and sex lamented this fresh invasion, but all my discomfort was gradually forgotten in the voluptuous thrill I felt when Henri came way up inside me . . . and flooded my itching sex with his hot discharge. 'She's a passionate little bitch,' he gasped as he drew his weapon out, and in truth I could feel the lips of my slit open and close in sensuous desire as the warm tip of his prick evaded them.

"And then Robert began to breathe faster and faster

and jerk furiously to and fro, until all of a sudden he came and my mouth was filled with hot sperm. I had not expected this, but he seemed to derive the greatest pleasure as he thrust his thigh up against my face until his sex hair tickled my lips, and in a husky voice told me to swallow. I blushed with shame at this fresh demand, but he simply would not withdraw, and I realized that I could not hold my breath much longer. So I gulped . . . and swallowed . . . and then there was only a warm salty taste in my mouth which was not too unpleasant.

" 'Now it's my turn!' exclaimed Henri, pushing Robert aside. As he had just spent between my thighs his prick was quite limp and he told me to take it in my mouth and suck and tongue it till it stiffened up again. As a matter of fact my sucking caresses had an almost instant effect, so I tickled him with my tongue and shook my head passionately from side to side until he came, and my mouth was once more filled with pulsing love juice. After such a succession of indecencies I felt sure I would be released, for it seemed as if nothing more could be expected of me. But the boys' ingenuities were by no means fully exhausted.

"They untied my legs . . . I was too tired to kick when they did so . . . and placed my feet flat on the bed beside my buttocks, in a way that parted my knees and offered my cunt . . . as I thought more fully to their attack. Then they fetched a shaving stick and wet it in my spend and soaped my buttocks and the crevice in between until they were all slippery, and then they did the same to my bottom-hole itself. Before I knew what was happening the tip of the stick slipped in. It

31

hurt a little and the soap stung until I squeezed with my rump as one does on another occasion, and a really exciting sensation began to go through me . . . spreading out from my bottom in every direction.

"I felt so ashamed of enjoying it that I tightened all my muscles in an involuntary movement which made the stick slip right out, and I blushed with confusion at such an embarrassing gesture.

" 'Now she is ready for it, the sexy little bitch!' said Robert, as he held my knees further apart. Henri pushed a pillow under my buttocks so as to raise them still more, and then got between my legs and thrust his swelling penis down at my little back entrance.

" 'No! No! Not in there!' I gasped, as I endeavored to wriggle free. 'Put it in the front way if you want to, and I'll promise to be good, but please don't try and get it in there. It's too tight, you just can't get it in!'

"But I was wrong and he could get it in. I screamed once as he pushed down harder, but after it was inside and thrusting to and fro it gave me the strangest feeling, even more exciting than when it was in my slit. I must admit that I came sooner than he did, and I flooded the bed and everything dreadfully. And then when he drew his penis out the two of them rolled me over on my face and Robert mounted me and began to fuck my tight little bottom from the back door, so to speak. They fingered my slit and squeezed my breasts while he did this, and for the sake of appearances I continued to protest, but in reality I was so hot by this time that I wanted to be attacked anywhere and everywhere at once. The weight of Robert's body parted my rounded buttocks as his penis thrust in between them and deep into my bottom . . . I could feel it going in and in and in. And his balls were swinging to and fro between my legs as he fucked in and out of my quivering body.

"'Go on! Go on!' I gasped, as I raised my buttocks to meet his thrusts, and rubbed them amorously against his thighs. 'Push it right in! All the way up! I've never been . . . had . . . like this before! Henri! Tickle me from the front while he does it! Quick! Ohh! Ohh! Your fingers are right inside now! Ohhh! Ohhh! Robert is all the way up me now! I think he's coming! Do you want to come too? Come closer and let me kiss it! How big it is! Ohh! Ohhh! Ohhhhh!'"

Clara closed the book, it was the end of the chapter, and laid it down on the bed, hoping that her blushes were not too evident. While she had been reading Conrad had been touching her more and more familiarly, his fingers caressing whatever part of her body she mentioned, including her bottom-hole, and rubbing his prick against her thighs from time to time. Her legs had spread apart long before this, and he was caressing her between her thighs, plucking at the pink lips of her sex, and even with his forefinger tickling her clitoris, at the top of the soft red groove that even the curls of her sex-hair did not hide.

She was in an agony of humiliation, the picture of utter misery and shame. She looked so young and crushed . . . and quite bewildered to find herself in such a predicament.

"Let me feel your bottom now, Clara," he whispered softly. "It looks so deliciously white and soft and tempting."

"You have been feeling it, haven't you?" she murmured, but she obediently turned on her side as he pushed her in that direction, and offered him her pert little rear from the back, so that he could caress her buttocks with their firm young curve and tickle with his fingers in the shadowy cleft . . . where it was plentifully wetted with the juice that had run down from her cunt while she was reading and being fingered. She covered her face with both hands as he poked at her behind, and her shoulders quivered when he took his finger out of her bottom and placed it in the crack of her cunt.

"You're not going to do anything to me, are you?" Clara's voice was shot with fright. She turned her blue eyes up to him beseechingly, and pleaded with a single word. "Please?"

He had had enough of bending her defenses and shaming her, at least for tonight. Actually fucking her could wait, for after he had once possessed her she would never be very ashamed again.

"No!" he promised her. "I'm not gong to do anything more to you now. I only wanted to see if you could make any sacrifice which might be demanded of you if you are to find your sister."

"Then may I put my clothes on now?" Clara asked timidly.

"Why, of course," he said. "I'm going now, and you must try and not worry about your sister. I'm sure she's all right and will turn up again soon."

34

He kissed her on both eyes and then on the mouth. "Now you can go off in a corner and have a good cry," he told her. He knew, somehow, that when he was gone she would do just that, and it gave him a pleasant sense of superiority to know that so innocent a girl would cry just because he had made her undress in front of him, and then lie with him on the bed while he had played with her naked body and sex, and he was glad to think that she would be crying and remembering him after he had gone.

Chapter 3

She draws her chair around the corner of your desk, for it is important to her that you get a good view of her lovely legs, and she says: "Mister District Attorney . . ." Her red hair spreads around her head like a halo, and she lies to you like an angel.

"I never had much to do with Maxie," she says. "I guess I was mixed up with the wrong people, that's all. I never knew about the gas filling stations and the counterfeit money that was passed there. I didn't think anything of the fact that all the time he was giving me new tens to spend. Really I didn't. You do believe me, don't you, Mister District Attorney?"

She draws her skirt a bit higher and crosses her knees, so that you get a good peek at white flesh above her stocking tops. The fan which is blowing hot air around the room to cool it off on this hot afternoon ruffles her white blouse against her figure . . . drawing your eyes to the bare slim throat. She leans forward toward you in an encouraging gesture, and her breasts strain maturely against her black shirt-waist, so cool and crinkly against her white suit.

You have to give her credit, she has a quick eye for the direction of your gaze, and she's as anxious as can be to oblige you wherever possible. You look far down into her blouse through the transparent silk, and the two swelling mounds on display are really gorgeous.

These call girls have what it takes, and they know how to dress it up.

"I know I've been a silly girl," she says. She gives you a quick glance from beneath the eyebrows she uses so well, and then adds: "You know, Daddy would have spanked me for being so stupid . . . when I was a little girl! In fact I guess he would have done it right now, if he were still alive!" The trim white skirt slips a little higher as she says this, but she does not seem to notice how much bare leg she has on display.

"So you think you ought to be spanked?" comes back the District Attorney, toying with a paper knife and glancing at the full line of her rounded white thigh. Her skirt is drawn tight against the upper curve of it, one would imagine that a hand skillfully applied there would produce a fine resounding smack, and he smiles slightly at the idea, as he looks at her quizzical face.

"Don't you think so too?" she asks coyly, smiling up at him coquettishly. That smile would play hell with a jury, though maybe the women wouldn't fall for it.

"So you want me to play daddy, do you? You wouldn't by any chance be trying to bribe the law to see how hot that little behind can get if it's spanked, would you?"

You reach out suddenly and pinch her thigh, but she doesn't move her leg away, only makes her eyes bigger. You can see her calculating whether to register coy surprise or lascivious warm promise. Her purse drops to the floor and she reaches out to pick 'it up . . . stretching her leg out toward you, the one your hand is resting on. You can feel the muscles under the bare flesh, and you slip your hand right up under her skirt.

37

"Come here and sit in my lap!" you bid her. She's certainly a prompt little kitten. Her buttocks are warm and spreading when posed on your thighs, and she puts a soft arm around your neck, pressing her taut breasts up to your face. Your hand fits itself to one of her plump buttocks, and you squeeze the softly yielding mound. You raise her skirt and look at the lovely line of her naked legs, and the laciness of her gossamer panties. You open her bra and admire her pink tipped breasts, the nipples of which are as hard as two red cherries.

"I'm going to spank you just as your daddy would, you little bitch," you tell her. And you push her off your lap with a gentle touch that belies your rough speech of a moment ago. You clear the odds and ends from the top of your desk in a few seconds, and turn back to her. "Come on, lift up your skirt and let's see what you've got underneath it!"

You look at her as she stands there, holding up her clothes with both hands, and not looking a bit scared. You tell her to turn around and let you see the moon that's going to be spanked. She has a small bottom really, but she's petite herself, so it appears to be full and round. It thrusts out pinkly, and the breeze from the window flutters her panties. You saunter over and lock the room door, telling her to take down her panties only part way. She'd take them off and throw them out of the window if you said so, but you just want them below her buttocks, at the curve of her thighs, they look much more attractive that way than a bare bottom does.

"Now bend over the desk," you tell her. You push

her head a bit lower, and she rests it on her purse and grasps the edge of the desk with both hands, and her feet lift from the floor as she does so. You fondle the delicate naked bottom for just a moment, and then your palm fetches it a resounding smack! The white flesh reddens in an instant under the blow, and the twin mounds jerk and quiver voluptuously on the rebound. The mere sensuality of the scene delights you.

"Ooooooh!" she gasps. Not from coyness but from shock. You didn't hurt her much but you really did surprise her. If she's going to yell at each smack you'll have to send Jackson out to lunch or something. But she promises to be quiet. She says she knows she deserves a good spanking, and that she won't make a sound. The lace panties flutter and the heels fly up with each smack. She reacts very prettily to a spanking. You don't really hurt her, but on each buttock there is a red blush, and you go on spanking her for quite a time because, as you tell her, she has been such a bad girl.

You notice that your cock is as stiff as a poker by now. It proves quite exciting to paddle a girl's fanny like this, for her cunt shows up every time your hand smacks and her heels fly up in the air. She doesn't yell any more, but her breath comes with a little gasp between her teeth as she reacts to the blows.

There's something wonderfully and even indecently amusing about a bare-bottomed girl in a modern office. Steel files and desks and efficiency everywhere, and in the midst of it a pretty little piece with her skirt up and her panties down, showing everything she's got. When you've finished spanking this one you go to the cooler for a drink of water, and stand there and watch her complacently. She poses there, with her trim skirt all ruffled up and her face flushed, biting her lip and holding her clothes up for you to have a last look at her.

Very deliberately you go over to her and tell her to unbutton your pants and take your cock out. She fumbles for a minute with your fly and then pulls it out, and you certainly look a little odd with it posed there against your well-pressed trousers and smart jacket. She looks at it calculatingly and then up at you, probably speculating whether it will fit her. So you tell her to lie down again on her face, and she obeys meekly. You stand there in between her legs, slapping your cock gently across her buttocks. She evidently likes the feel of it on her bare behind, and it probably tickles her a bit where it touches her naked flesh, for she turns her head and gives you a twinkling, dirty wink of pleasure, and then jiggles her soft buttocks at you invitingly.

What a sweet little bitch she is. You look down at the line of her pink slit, and slide a finger along her yielding cunt, all wet already with anticipation.

She likes that pretty well, even if it does tickle, for she wriggles and clutches the edge of the desk for dear life. In fact she's as hot as hell already. Now she really wants it, and she shoves her buttocks back and reaches for your cock with her gaping cunt lips. You slide the tip in very gently through the wet lips, and she sucks it right into her hole before you know what's happened. She lets out her breath with an ecstatic gasp. Then suddenly she giggles and a faint blush shows as she mur-

murs: "Daddy would never have done anything like this to me, and you know it!" And she wiggles her ass back at you in mock triumph as she feels you drive deeper in.

"You'd better make this the fuck of your life," you tell her. "You're trying to fuck away a five year jail sentence right now, young lady."

Even her self-esteem can't make her believe that she has got anything between her legs worth that much. But you have to admit that she tries as hard as she damn well can. She rolls her bottom around as though she were made of rubber, she really isn't holding back a thing, and you feel that your cock's up further in her cunt than anyone has been in a long time.

"If you want me to do anything else," she gasps, "just tell me and I'll do it. Do you want me again tonight? Or any time? You can fuck me . . . or give it to me any way at all. . . ."

She literally means it. Spank her, fuck her, suck her, give her your ass to kiss, she wants anything right now. You hold her by the hip with one hand and reach the other around to tickle her slit from the front. She twists and moans with her passion, and you can feel the love juice wetting all the inside of her thighs. Tickle her with your cock and then shove it right up her. In! In! The crisis overtakes you both, and your sperm jets up into her at the moment her spend floods down over your cock and balls.

You fall back into a chair, and she stands up and looks at you, mutely asking permission to lower her skirt over her bare legs. The telephone begins to ring, and you pick it up, while the girl . . . getting no answer to her pleading look . . . sinks to her knees in front of your chair and begins to suck your cock into comparative rigidity again.

"This is Clara Reeves," a clear voice says. "I just got some news on that matter which may be important. I'd better see you this evening, and then I'll be able to tell you about it." The receiver is replaced with a click as she finishes, and you look down at the half-naked girl crouched down at your feet, still waiting to see if there are any more demands for her to carry out in order to satisfy you.

She is running her tongue daintily along your cock, holding it like a stick of asparagus in her fingers, and just nibbling at the tip. She puts it right in between her lips and smiles up at you mischievously as she sucks it in and in and in, pressing her red lips down on the bare flesh. Her lipstick is marking your cock, and that's rather amusing. She is softly squeezing your balls and running an insinuating finger down between your buttocks. You slide forward in your chair so as to let her slip her finger up your behind. She twists the finger in slowly so as not to hurt you, and then titillates the flesh while she sucks you into a proud rigidity.

You wonder about the phone call and what Clara has discovered. Then you look down at the little red-head, still kneeling at your feet, and dragging her wet mouth up your cock and pressing it down with an expert side to side movement of her head. You let your mind slide as she goes faster and faster and your hips jerk up and down spasmodically.

Her hands poke and squeeze your balls and ass-hole all the while her lips move and her tongue flicks around the tip of your cock in circles, faster and faster. You gasp and spend in a perfect flood in her mouth, and she gulps it down as if she liked it, kneading your balls and twisting her finger in your hole all the while.

Time passes and you sit up and open your eyes. She is idly drawing down on your cock with her soft lips, running her tongue very gently round the tip. She is still sitting on the floor at your feet, with one hand resting on your thigh

"You might as well get up now," you tell her, patting her bare behind

"You're sure you don't want anything more?" she asks, as she gets to her feet and lets fall her skirt so as to cover her nakedness.

"No, I couldn't take any more now. I've got to go downtown, anyway Fix yourself up so that you can make a good snappy exit."

So she stands there and slips on her panties. You can't quite remember when she took them off. Must have been before you fucked her, anyway. She performs miracles of adjustment with a mirror and vanity box from her bag. Everything about her is trim. She pins back her hair where it was tousled by her spanking. And then she touches up her lips with rouge foncé, for after all her recent program was vigorous enough to ruin any girl's lipstick. An eyebrow pencil is really an unnecessary item, but she uses one, and then feels equal to any emergency.

"I feel so much better now," she says. "I feel just the way I used to feel when I'd been naughty and had it on my conscience, and then after Daddy gave me a first class spank on my bare behind I knew everything was all right again. But his spankings never made me feel the way I felt this afternoon, I must say." And she gives you a roguish smile to see how you like it.

"How soon do you think you'll deserve another spanking?" you ask her. You are still thinking of the round buttocks, still pink and just a bit sore under the tight white skirt that hides them. She's going down to the street now with your spanking and your fucking still with her, and your sperm still salty on her sexy-looking lips.

You wonder how she feels about having other men looking at her lips and breasts and bottom just after you have had them. She doesn't pause in her adjustments, but bends so as to straighten the seam of her stocking. "Whenever you think that I need one!" she says in answer to your query.

"So it's a permanent arrangement, is it? I go on spanking you and laying you on my office desk whenever I feel like it, and you go on handing out counterfeit money any time you feel like it?" you say caustically, and watch her pretty face to see how she takes it.

"Oh, but Mister District Attorney!" she objects, wide eyes on you, in pretended astonishment. You are back just where you were before she took her panties down, and she shows dismay at her sudden discovery.

"I never knew anything about the money, you know that I didn't! And what we did this afternoon, I didn't mean . . . I really wanted to do that . . . to have your big thing way up inside me . . . any time at all I want it . . ." she protests sadly.

"All right! All right! Run along now! And come up

and see me on Thanksgiving Day, maybe!" you tell her hastily.

"Oh! Mister District Attorney! Thank you so much!" she twinkles as the door opens and shuts behind her. In a moment it opens again and she pushes an impudent face around the edge. "Thanksgiving Day is two whole weeks yet!" she points out to you, reprovingly. "I might get into mischief if I don't see you before then. I guess I just need a spanking from time to time to make me stay good!"

Chapter 4

C lara was terribly excited when Conrad met her that evening at ten o'clock. She had no sooner shown him into the house than she burst out with it and announced: "I've met part of the gang that work with the Scorpion, I'm sure I have, so what do you think of that, Conrad?" They were already well past the Mr. Garnett stage, so they sat side by side on the couch while she related everything that had happened to her during the day.

"A woman called me on the phone," her story began, "and she said that the ring we advertised about belonged to a friend of hers. Well, I met her at the Clive Hotel. She calls herself Mrs. Mason, and I guess that's her name all right. She's in her early thirties and very pretty. She has dark hair and eyes and a deep husky voice that sounds very cultured. And she has the tiniest feet I ever saw."

Conrad smiled at her in appreciation. Clara had certainly enjoyed herself, and picked up all the thrills to be had.

"She didn't say anything about the ring right away," Clara went on. "We took a table at the Clive and ordered tea and cakes and she was very pleasant to me. Before I realized it she had asked me to come out and visit her at her country place some weekend. We both talked about all sorts of things before she even asked me about the ring. But when I told her I didn't have it with me she seemed a little disappointed, so I asked her if she would come home with me and get it. But she said she had to meet a friend and couldn't. And instead, she asked me if it would be all right if her brother-in-law went with me to get it instead, and I said yes. So she made a phone call and presently a man came and joined us at the table. She introduced him as John Webster, and said that he'd drive out with me and get the ring.

"Mrs. Mason and the Webster man were very friendly, and I got the impression that he might have been an old flame of hers and anyhow I didn't believe he was any relative at all. And from what I found out about him later, boy friend or not, he probably knows her much too well. That's my impression.

"We finished tea finally and Mrs. Mason wanted to know if I could come out to her place in the country tomorrow. So I promised to phone her tonight and let her know if I was coming or not . . . she said I could call her any time after eleven . . . and then I got into the Webster man's car with him . . .

"He seemed all right, but he persisted in paying me all sorts of silly compliments all the time. Very personal ones, too. All about my . . . bosom and things like that. But he didn't do anything else until we arrived here and were in the house. Then, when I had given him the ring, and we were sitting here having a drink, he suddenly came over to where I was sitting and put his arms around me.

"I hardly knew what to do. So I just sat still, and he ran his hands all over my arms and back while he

47

kissed me. I let him go on kissing me, and I opened my mouth when he seemed to want me to while he was kissing me, and then he made me lean back in my chair while he felt my breasts. I was a bit scared by this time, but I didn't know if he was the Scorpion or not, though I didn't think so, and I was quite determined not to seem scared or surprised, so I just smiled at him to encourage him. I wanted these people to think I was their type, so that I could get mixed up with them and find out about Rita. Was that right?"

Conrad nodded sagely. "He was probably just testing you out. So then after he felt your breasts and you smiled back at him, what did he do?"

"He slipped his hand under my dress. I hated to have him touch me there. I didn't really like him at all. But I kept on smiling and pretending that this was just what I wanted. So he suggested we come over here on the couch. Once we were on the couch together he became very eager and insistent. He began to fondle my legs, and put his hands right up between my thighs, and then he asked me if a man had ever . . . had me? I told him 'no' and winked at him, so that he wouldn't guess whether I meant it or not.

"And then he told me that if I wanted to be made love to, and he obviously couldn't imagine any girl not wanting that . . . I ought positively to go to one of Mrs. Mason's weekend parties. But that I should look him up first. And then he began feeling my thighs again. So I felt sure it wouldn't be long before he'd want me to take my dress off, the way you said, and it certainly wasn't. He had been pushing my skirt up

48

along my legs so that he could feel between them, and while he was pulling up my dress he was pushing me down on the couch with his shoulder, and then finally I was lying down altogether."

Clara paused, and appeared reluctant to continue. "What's the matter?" asked Conrad. "Have you forgotten what happened?"

"No!" she said, shaking her head and turning crimson with embarrassment. "I haven't forgotten a thing that happened to me then."

"He made you take your dress off, didn't he?" Conrad asked her.

"Yes!" said Clara, blushing once more. "He made me take my dress off, and everything else besides . . . my stockings and my undies and everything. . . ."

"Was this while you were lying on the couch?" he queried.

"Partly while I was on the couch," said Clara. "And then he made me stand up in front of him while I took the rest of my clothes off, until I was all bare!"

"And then you had to lie down again with him . . . naked?"

"Yes, that's right. I had to lie down with him . . . naked. It was almost . . . I don't mean to sound as if I was putting you both in the same class, I didn't like him at all . . . he wasn't a bit nice . . . but otherwise it was almost like it was last night with you. What he did, I mean. I had to lie in his arms while he fingered me and felt every part of my body. Every single part."

"You mean he looked at your cunt too?" inquired Conrad.

Clara swallowed hard. "Yes, there too. He made me spread my legs apart, and let him feel me there, and touch me, and then he put his finger right inside."

"And he still had his clothes on?"

"He did then, but he took them off right after that. He made me sit up, and he wouldn't let me cover my breasts with my hands, and he made me watch him while he undressed. He made me tell him that I had never seen a naked man, and it seemed to delight him like anything to be the first man I ever saw nude. He particularly wanted me to say that the hair over his . . . thing surprised me. . . ." Clara paused and blushed slightly. "But I said no . . . it didn't, because I had hair there too. He looked a little sore about that. And then he came back to the couch with me. . . ." She smiled shyly as she noticed that Conrad was laughing over her last sally, and then went on with her story. "And then he stood up in front of me and made me touch him. He took my hand and put it on his . . . on his . . . oh, do I have to tell you all of this?" She flushed deeply and looked down at the floor in her embarrassment.

"If it would be any easier . . ." said Conrad. He got up and put out all the lights but one in the far corner, and then he came back to join Clara on the couch again. "If you can't tell me . . . then show me. Where did you have to put your hand?"

Clara reached out with her hand and timidly touched the front of his trousers. "Right there!" she faltered.

"He made you touch his prick, then?" said Conrad.

"And that wasn't all," she concurred. "He not only made me touch it, but he made me hold it in my hand

and watch it grow big and stiff, while the skin at the top stretched and became shiny till it looked more like a plum and less like a strawberry, the way it had looked at first."

She stopped short, as if she had suddenly realized that she had been very attentive to appearances for the unwilling innocent that she was supposed to be. "And then he made me hold it in my palm and . . . and . . ." she made a vague up and down gesture.

"Do what?" asked Conrad with an air of bewilderment. "If you don't mind I think you'd better show me just what you mean. I can see you don't like to say it right out loud. Go ahead and show me. I won't look at your face while you do it."

Clara couldn't believe at first that he was serious, but he nodded at her questioning look, and she bent in a confusion of blushes and fumbled with his trouser buttons. "Oh! Conrad!" she exclaimed, as his fly opened, "I'm so ashamed of myself. I did something so dirty today that I can't believe that it was I who did it. . . ."

"Yes?" he queried, and stifled the impulse to add, "and here you are doing it again." He could see that something had happened to shame her, and felt inclined to point out that it was part of the price which she would have to pay to find her sister if she were in earnest.

Silently Clara opened his fly and fumbled with his underwear. She took out his prick very gingerly, and held it like a hot potato, passing it lightly from one hand to the other. It was already warm to the touch and stiffening in her grasp. She moved her hand gently to and fro, illustrating the manner in which she had been obliged to manipulate it. Bigger and bigger it grew under her caressing fingers, and Clara moved her hand up and down on it faster and faster.

"He made me do it faster," she confessed, "and he grew very excited. He seemed to be trying to pull my head toward him. And at last I wouldn't do it any longer. My wrist was so tired, but I didn't tell him that was why I stopped. That was when he lay down beside me the second time."

The D.A. took Clara by the hand and closed her fingers more firmly round his prick, which she had almost released as she was speaking. "He was feeling me . . . there . . ." Clara said. Conrad had slipped his hand right under her dress and into her crotch. He was a little surprised to find that today she did not have any panties on. "He was doing everything you did there with your fingers," Clara went on, "and he made me play with his . . . prick . . . again." She illustrated how she had held it, and she moved her slim fingers along the stiffened shaft and then around his balls in exact detail.

"And weren't you ashamed?" suggested Conrad softly.

"Oh! Yes, I was horribly ashamed. But I had to do it. And he wasn't so well-made as you are either, and I didn't get a bit excited doing it." Clara blushed, but continued with her story. "He said he didn't know whether he would . . . would fuck me or not, but that perhaps if I did what I was doing well enough, he wouldn't have to. So I did everything he told me to just as he told me to. I pulled it and I rubbed it and I took his balls in my other hand and squeezed them gently. And I let him touch me and tickle me as much as he wanted. I was afraid that if I stopped he would really . . . fuck me . . . so I pretended to be enjoying myself very much. When he asked me how I liked it I said that I had never felt anything like it in my life."

"And that was true, wasn't it?" the D.A. chuckled, as he worked his finger in and out more insistently in Clara's yielding slit. "I suppose he was doing just about what I'm doing?" he added.

"He was using two fingers," Clara confessed shyly.

Conrad made the amendment as she opened her legs a bit to accommodate his action. "How long did this go on?" he asked her after a few minutes. They had been lying side by side in silence, diligently caressing each other's genitals.

"Just about as long as we've been doing it," sighed Clara, as she rubbed her forefinger over the red tip of the cock she was caressing so fondly. "And then suddenly. . . ."

"Suddenly this happened . . ." Conrad finished for her in a choked voice. The girl's hand was suddenly full of warm sperm, and the bud of his cock was spurting and spurting. . . .

"Ohh! Conrad, how could you? You didn't even warn me," cried Clara, wiping her fingers on the handkerchief she had snatched from his breast pocket. She looked at him accusingly: "You're just as mean as he was. I didn't expect this of you!"

Suddenly the young girl began to cry on his shoulder, and he took her in his arms again. "I just hate it, and I hate myself for doing it, and causing those kind of feelings in men. Even you feel that way toward me. I wish I were dead."

"There! There! There's no need to cry!" Conrad soothed her. He caressed her cunt and breasts very softly, and after a bit she calmed down. It was curious, he thought, how any kind of violent emotions made a woman more sexy. Clara was breathing more deeply now, shorter and shorter, and her thighs were opening and closing on his hand in uncontrollable and furious excitement, and suddenly her love juice flooded down onto his caressing fingers and relaxed legs in a perfect deluge as she blushingly turned her lips up to find his eager mouth.

Chapter 5

"*I*'d have sent someone to meet you if I'd known about it earlier," apologized Mrs. Mason, as she drew Clara into the front seat of the car. "But when we have a real party I always send the servants away, so I couldn't get the car for a little while."

"You're having a lot of people then?" the girl asked, as the car turned onto the highway and began to pick up speed.

"With you that makes thirty, I think. I always like a party with plenty of people, it's so much more interesting to be able to explore different personalities." Mrs. Mason stopped the car as she spoke, and proceeded to unlock some lodge gates which opened onto a long, shady driveway. Then the house came into view, big and Spanish-looking, with several people in slacks and shorts lolling on the shady veranda.

A man collected Clara's bag from the car, led her in through the hallway and upstairs to her room, where he vanished before she could even thank him. So as soon as she had unpacked her things and put them away in the scented drawers of the bureau, Clara went downstairs again to explore the situation.

She went out onto the terrace, and suddenly she caught sight of John Webster talking to a young girl in slacks. "Oh, there you are," she called. She was actually glad to see him, although on the previous day she had been positive she never wanted to see him again. But he seemed like a temporary refuge from the dark unknown just then.

"I hoped you'd turn up," he said, as he led her down the terrace and into the garden. To Clara it seemed that there must be many more than thirty people at Mrs. Mason's weekend party. Wherever she looked she seemed to see amorous couples embracing. They lay under the trees in shady spots, and there was no doubt as to what they were doing. Clara hadn't been sure whether the girl on the boy's lap on the porch had been fucking, though she rather thought so.

But out here on a beach chair a man was lying with a girl curled up between his legs, calmly sucking him off, while a boy and a girl nearby watched them and offered advice and hearty encouragement. The girl between the man's legs had only the halter of her bathing suit on, and her cunt pouted openly from her curled up thighs in back.

"It's all very . . . free, isn't it?" stammered Clara.

"What? Oh, that?" His eyes flickered over the scene that had attracted her attention. "They're only doing what they want to, and that's the first rule at Mrs. Mason's parties. The second is not to pretend that you came here to do it with your own husband or wife. Sensible, isn't it? If a man is jealous he can stay at home and keep his wife there too. If he comes here, it shows he's looking for some fresh cunt, so why shouldn't his wife have a change too?"

"But aren't they in love with each other?" Clara asked. Webster just laughed, so she tried a new tack.

"But does everyone come here to make love?" she went on.

"Mainly that, I suppose!" he replied. "Or else to take drugs or see dirty pictures or do whatever else interests them most. This is a private world where everyday rules are out. And since love is the one thing most firmly restricted in the world outside, there's bound to be quite a lot of it unrestricted around here. Sex as a fine art is how I should describe it. Ask anybody around if you want details as to procedure, and you'll probably get more information than you bargained for."

Clara let that opening pass, and walked to the house with him, feeling that she had made herself look slightly silly. As they passed the green tiled swimming pool she remarked a bit caustically, "At least they don't swim in the nude, as far as I can see."

"Swim naked?" queried John Webster, "no, not in the daytime anyhow. But I think clothes are somehow more interesting in daytime, especially when you think how few really handsome bodies there are except on very young girls."

"Do you mean on . . . or on top of?" Clara asked him with a bawdy daring that surprised even herself.

Webster looked surprised too, for a moment, and then gave a little laugh. "Well, you are improving, aren't you?" he said mockingly.

They were back in the house now, and he led her casually into a small drawing room that was deserted. There was a radio playing somewhere in the distance. Johnny sat down on the couch beside her and lit a cigarette.

Somehow she wasn't so frightened of him now when she thought of him as Johnny as she had been when he was John Webster. He was just a playboy now, and not menacing any more.

"How did you feel after your lesson yesterday?" he asked, and all the dangers that had threatened rushed back into Clara's mind as the blood rushed back to her cheeks.

"Must I have felt some particular way?" she temporized, while her cheeks flamed with embarrassment.

"No, I suppose not. But it would be polite to pretend that you did." His easy jocularity infuriated her.

"Well, I did feel something," she exclaimed, jumping up and stamping her small foot. "I felt ashamed and miserable. I wished that I were dead . . . or that you were dead."

Johnny pulled her around to face him, and taking hold of her leg above the knee forced her to sit down again on the sofa with her legs crossed over one of his and under the other one, so that she could scarcely move away from him. "That's no way to feel," he told her. "Or maybe it is, for a girl like you. Would you like me to make you feel miserable and ashamed again today? Do you like that?" He gave her a shrewd look which she failed to understand.

"Of course not," she said. "Don't be ridiculous!" She extricated her legs from his with some difficulty, and reached towards the table for a drink, just because it gave her something to do. They were both using the same glass, she realized with a shock. Oh, well, the alcohol would kill all the germs. Besides, he probably didn't have any germs. She hated him, of course, but he really was very clean and well-dressed.

"I think I'll give you another lesson, anyway," he told her. "I rather enjoyed that way of making you ashamed. Wouldn't you like to do what we were doing yesterday?" His hand was now creeping under her skirt just the way his voice was creeping under her skin. He tried to kiss her, but she hurriedly occupied her lips with the glass.

"You were very tempting with all your clothes off," he told her. "Very pretty indeed, especially those pink-tipped little breasts of yours." Clara felt her breasts swell and the nipples harden as his voice recalled them to her conscious mind, while a queer little flutter seized the muscles of her loins. "And the way you acted was very charming too, mainly because you thought you were being so wicked and couldn't help yourself, didn't you now?"

"Yes," said Clara in a small voice. "What we did yesterday was terribly wicked."

"Well, that's a matter of opinion," he replied. "But I'm glad you think so. And it would be just as wicked if we did it again, wouldn't it?"

"It would always be wrong," she replied seriously, feeling a little light-headed at the same time. "You did something very wrong with me yesterday." The little-girl sound of her voice surprised her.

"Well, I'm going to do it to you again!" he said.

He was already feeling her thighs, reaching up between her legs with quick fingers. She felt his hand slip inside her pants and for a moment she wondered whether girls who wore girdles were any safer from men's hands. "I don't suppose men try to feel up girls who wear girdles," she told herself silently, but at the same time she felt a little proud of her trim figure and her firm behind.

Suddenly she realized that Johnny's hand was on her slit and spreading apart the hair and the tender lips in a very deliberate but decided manner. She was about to object and pull away, when his hand came out from under her dress . . . but only for a moment . . . and then it returned from his mouth and was dipped under her skirt and seized her again. Clara gasped at the sudden thrill that went through her reluctant senses as his wetted finger slipped down through the folds of her tender sex.

His other arm slid round her waist, his fingers pressing into her belly. He turned her towards him and thrust against her so that she felt his swelling prick rubbing her thigh. She covered her face with her hands to hide her confusion. "Oh! No! Don't!" she said apprehensively. "Please don't."

Disregarding her entreaty he took her limp hand and put it on his sex. By this time his penetrating fingers were going, thrusting deeper and deeper into her cunt, from which the dew was already flowing. "Open your legs a little," he whispered. But she closed them tightly . . . on his hand.

"Now listen," he said, "take me to your room, or else I'll undress you right here on the sofa." His voice was heavy with passion. "I swear I'll make you do it right here where just anybody can see us if they come along. So you'd better come to your own room and let me take off your clothes and play with you just as we did yesterday."

60

She had no idea what a lovely ravished picture she made standing there with her hand hiding her face and her body drawn back as he pulled at her arm. She followed unsteadily behind him protesting, but afraid to protest too loudly. They went upstairs and she showed him the room Mrs. Mason had given her. He pushed her inside and closed the door after them.

"I don't want to do it," she cried, running across the room away from him, but unfortunately in the direction of the bed. "I just won't do it!" she gasped, as he picked her up and dropped her on the bed, ignoring her protests. He took off her shoes, and then rolled down her stockings over her slim legs, pinching her thighs as he did so. He made her raise her bottom while he pulled her skirt up past her hips, and then told her to sit up while he took it off over her head. He leaned toward her and reached back to unsnap her brassiere, disclosing twin breasts which rose and fell tumultuously with her exertions. To keep herself from falling backwards she put her arms around him, and he pushed her back gently on the bed and kissed her with hotly demanding lips.

Clara lay still while he pulled down her panties over her slender thighs. She kicked them off hopelessly, and they still hung on one ankle, so she left them there and covered her face and breasts with her crossed arms. Her legs had fallen apart, but she ignored that, for it seemed more important to her to hide her face. He compelled her to watch him while he undressed though. There were tears in her eyes, but she watched him, once more shocked by the strange potency of his throbbing prick that waved

61

slightly as he moved, couched as it was on his balls as he sat there on the bed next to her.

"Now play with my cock the way you did yesterday," said Johnny, as he closed her hand round his prick and made her do as he bid. The tears in her eyes overflowed and rolled down her cheeks. She felt so terribly humiliated by this act, but she kept his swelling sex in her hand and caressed it as he directed.

"Don't look away from it," he told her, lying back on the bed and drawing her nearer to him, while he closed her other hand on his balls. "I want you to see how wet you make it when you do that. Bend closer, don't be afraid of tangling your fingers in the hair." And poor Clara bent obediently to her task.

"And now I have something else for you," he exclaimed, springing off the bed suddenly. He made Clara get up and stand facing him on the rug. He pressed his body against hers and rubbed her belly with his cock. Her face only came to his shoulder, she discovered. He made her take his prick in both hands and rub her navel with it. She obeyed him sadly, at the same time wondering why she did so when she hated him so much. She wanted to cry. Tears stood in her eyes like diamonds as she rubbed the bud of his cock over her tender skin, and up and down the line of almost invisible hair that ran from her navel to her mount. He put his hands on her hips and caressed her buttocks while his cock poked into her navel and he bent her backwards toward the bed.

"Put it between your legs now," he ordered her. "Rub it in your cunt."

"I won't! Oh, no! I can't!" Clara was almost hysterical. She was helpless in his embrace. But still he didn't try to make her do it by sheer brute force. It wasn't rape, but it was hardly seduction either.

"I enjoy a certain amount of girlish resistance from you occasionally," he said, "but this is becoming tiresome. Perhaps you shouldn't have come to the party after all?"

She thought of Rita. More than anything else she wanted to find Rita. And Conrad would be so disappointed over her failure. So she relaxed in Webster's embrace, and held his cock between her legs, rubbing it in the depths of her black cunt-hair with her hands, and pressing her slit down against it in a diffident gesture of desire. The tip of his prick slipped in between the lips and she rubbed it up and down some more. It felt wet and sticky and terribly hot.

"That's better!" he said. He helped her with the rubbing by moving his hips too. The movement was circular by now, what with her hips and her hands all helping. Together they pressed and tickled with his prick inside the entrance to her cunt, and he made her look down and watch what her hands were doing.

"I'll teach you to like all of this before the weekend is over," he promised her as he pressed her back on the bed.

Clara could not resist saying it. "But I'll never like you," she murmured in a bitter whisper.

This seemed to infuriate him. "Kneel down!" he ordered her roughly.

"Kneel down? In front of you?" Clara was incredulous.

His voice became sharp and domineering. "Yes, right

down on your knees. Don't be bashful now . . . this isn't going to hurt you any more than the other things you've done."

She hated to have to face his prick, and it was so close to her face that its hairs were thrusting against her eyes and mouth. Slowly she sank back on her pink heels as she knelt. He made her take his cock in her hands again and begin to caress it once more.

"Do you know why I made you kneel?" Johnny demanded. He brushed back the hair which concealed her face, and looked into her eyes.

"No!" she whispered. It was almost a sob.

"Because I want you to kiss it. Yes, there!" He held her by the hair before she could rise, "Kiss it, Clara!" he said.

"Oh! No, I can't. Please don't make me, Johnny."

"If you don't I shall have to tell Mrs. Mason that you're here to spy on her," he threatened.

Clara's frightened start must have confirmed his suspicion that something was wrong somewhere. "How do you know why I'm here?" she whispered.

"I don't want to know why you're here, and I shan't try to find out if you do what I tell you," Johnny replied. "Now are you going to do as you're told?"

She wanted him to say something more, to disclose what were his intentions, but she knew he wouldn't. She realized she was in his power and she just nodded miserably.

"Will you do everything I say?" he demanded. "For as long as you're here, will you come to me whenever I tell you to, and undress . . . and do whatever I want you to?"

"I guess so!" she said humbly. "Is this the way your rule about only doing what you want to do works out?" she added.

Johnny grinned. "I am doing what I want to do," he said. The smile left his face, and he bent toward her until his cock brushed her cheek. "Suck it now," he ordered.

She turned her mouth to it dutifully and . . . but she just couldn't make her soft lips touch that big red sex.

"I can't, Johnny . . . I just can't," she stammered.

"You have to!" he ordered sternly. She managed to make her lips touch it, and then would have pulled away but that his fingers were twisted in her hair and prevented her. He pushed her mouth back into position. "With your tongue," he insisted, "don't just kiss it."

She forced herself to open her lips and her tongue just flicked across the red bud of his cock. The juice from it had a funny taste, she decided, and she made a wry face. "That's not enough," he said. "You must do better than that." And soon, under his orders, she was licking it with the whole of her hot tongue instead of the tip, and was sliding her lips up and down his sex with her head cocked birdlike to one side. His prick was soon all wet from her lips and tongue, but he made her keep on licking and lipping it.

"You're licking my cock, Clara," he said softly, "aren't you?" and he plucked at her dark hair insistently.

She accepted her shame, and went on caressing him.

"Well, aren't you?" he demanded. Clara nodded her head dumbly. "No, speak up," he insisted.

"Yes, I'm licking it," she said, and went back to doing it once more.

"I didn't hear you clearly, what did you say?" he once more demanded.

"I'm . . . I'm . . ." she burst into tears.

"Go on and say it. You're licking my prick, aren't you?"

"Yes!" she whispered in a smothered voice. "I'm licking your prick." The tears rolled unheeded down her cheeks. She couldn't have believed that the words would ever pass her lips, but they had. Her will to resist seemed broken. And when he said she could get up, she did so slowly and as though she were half asleep.

He laid her on the bed and knelt across her bosom. He made her press her breasts together and hold his penis in the groove between them. Then he bent forward and told her to lick it once more, until it was wet all over and he began to work it to and fro in its warm throbbing nest. Faster and faster his movements grew, until he began to breathe heavily and to clutch at her naked shoulders. Suddenly his hips jerked wildly in a spasm of desire, and in another moment he came in a hot discharge which flooded her bosom and throat. By the time she realized what had happened, he had gotten up from the bed and was already dressing himself.

As soon as he had left the room she rushed to the bathroom, with her breasts jumping and jiggling wildly, and then scrubbed them off with soap and water . . . hurting herself with the washrag's roughness. She liked the hurt, it seemed in some way to ease her inner pain. She rinsed her mouth out again and again, and then went back to bed and began to cry softly and hopelessly.

Chapter 6

When she woke up again it was almost dusk. She dressed herself in a pretty lavender silk gown, and wandered out into the hall with its empty rooms and open doors. There were so many bedrooms that it seemed impossible that they should all be occupied. And at the end of the hall was one room with its door closed. So Clara's feminine curiosity impelled her to open it and peep inside. It was empty too, but was at least twice as large as the other rooms and contained an enormous bed covered in black satin. There was a canopy over it, and when Clara came closer she discovered that there was a mirror set in the top, the purpose of which it took her several moments to realize.

"I'd be too ashamed," she whispered to herself, seeing phantom shapes imaged in the mirror, with their sexes perversely joined. "Does the mirror magnify too, I wonder?" she added with a chuckle.

She wandered across the room to examine more closely some pictures on the wall in an alcove. She was so engrossed in them that she hardly heard the door open, and then she realized that there was someone else in the room with her. Standing back in the shadows she hesitated to announce her presence. A man and a girl had entered without noticing her, and

68

she hoped that they would perhaps leave again without the necessity of explaining herself.

But it soon became evident that they had no intention of leaving shortly. "Close the door," said the girl as the man followed her across the room with the evident intention of seeking a kiss. "And you'd better lock it too," she added. "You never know who might come wandering in at the critical moment and put us off." She was slightly older than Clara and perhaps prettier, wearing a white skirt and sweater with a college name on it in red. She unfastened the black belt at her waist and threw it on a chair. Then Clara realized that these people were not here just for a moment, and while she debated as to whether she should disclose her presence to them the opportunity was again lost.

The girl pulled the sweater off over her head. The weave of the wool had left its mark on her bare breasts, and she rubbed them briskly with her palms. The man came over and stood there fondling her bosom. He suddenly lifted her, still with her skirt and stockings on, and literally threw her onto the bed. She laughed. The man took off his polo shirt and trousers and the girl slipped out of her skirt with one lithe movement. She left her shoes and stockings on, scuffing the satin cover of the bed with her high heels.

"I knew you weren't wearing anything under your pants," the girl said. "I could see the head of your prick right through your trousers."

"So you were looking at it, were you?" the man mocked.

"Of course I was, and at every other man's cock too. I was wondering how much longer I could hold out without it in me!"

Clara gasped under her breath at the phrase that fell so casually from the other girl's lovely lips.

"I wanted to come up here all the afternoon," the girl mused while the man kicked off his shoes. "You were teasing me, damn you. You know how hot I get while I'm waiting to be fucked and all the rest of it."

"It hasn't hurt you to wait," the man answered. He took off the girl's shoes and then put them back on again. "You look more sexy in just shoes and stockings than any other girl I know," he added.

"I'm a sexy bitch, aren't I?" the girl replied, smiling up at him as she pulled him closer to her. "Next time I won't wait for you, I'll just go and fuck with whoever wants me." She took his prick in her hands as he lay beside her, and fondled it gently. "You know how hot I get when I think strange men are going to fuck me, especially if there's more than one of them."

Clara blushed crimson at her outspoken language.

The man felt between the girl's legs and she opened them wide. They curled toward each other, head to heels, and began their caresses. The girl held his cock between her palms as though she were praying. Then she began to twirl it, putting her lips to its bud and licking up the sperm that came to its throbbing tip.

The man exclaimed, and the girl suddenly jumped from the bed. "Wait! Wait!" she cried. She ran to a chest by the wall, her head not a yard from Clara's, and when she came back Clara saw she was carrying a cat-of-nine-tails like the one she had found in her sister's drawer.

The girl threw herself face down on the bed again, and reached out the whip to the man. "Go ahead!" she cried wildly. "Beat me! Hard! Hard!" She threw her legs apart so that her cunt gaped widely between them, and waited for him to strike. The whip whistled in the air and bit into the tender flesh of her back and loins. She quivered and then laughed. Clara saw her cunt flash as it caught the light where it was dripping wet from excitement. There was no question about it, but Clara found it hard to believe that being whipped could really get the girl so hot.

The whip fell once more across the girl's buttocks and they trembled and quivered. Then the man began to beat her in real earnest and Clara was amazed, for the girl laughed out loud, a laugh of real pleasure and not of hysteria. The lash was falling between her thighs now, and suddenly it flicked the lips of her sex and drew blood. At this moment the man's prick, which had been stiffly erect the whole time, began to spurt forth in great jets . . . and he ceased beating her. The girl whirled and flung her arms round his waist, opening her mouth to catch his spend as it jetted forth, and getting it all over her face and even in her hair.

Then she rolled over on her back and flung her legs wide apart, exposing her quivering cunt and begging the man to take her at once where she lay. Clara was horrified as she watched the amorous scene, but she had a guilty realization that her own sex was dripping with excitement too. "Oh! Please!" she found herself whispering under her breath, "don't let it excite me so dreadfully. I don't want to be like that too."

By now the man had thrown aside the whip and flung himself down on top of the frantically writhing girl on the bed. He turned her over and thrust in between her legs. She threw them high in the air in an ecstasy of passion and then dropped them over his shoulders, her body bent double like a jackknife. Their arms and legs seemed inextricably entangled and they both began to laugh.

The man's throbbing weapon drove down into the girl's cunt, deeper and deeper, and Clara could see her buttocks become wet and shiny with love juice as the invader thrust in and out of her slit with a sucking noise, and her lover's balls swung and bounced against her frantically jerking bottom. It seemed only after a moment that he spent furiously, and the girl lowered one leg to encircle his waist and draw him closer as she panted in ecstasy that she was coming, too.

Clara was far more exhausted than either of the two participants in the amorous encounter she had witnessed. The man took a corner of the sheet and wiped the moisture from the girl's back and behind, and they both left the room without discovering that they had had a witness to their love match.

As she too tried to leave the room, Clara found that she could hardly stand. Her thighs were dripping wet and she pretended that it was perspiration and tucked her skirt in between them to wipe it off. She was wearing no petticoat, and the love juice stained the silk of her dress immediately. She left the room as if in a dream, and did not return to reality until she found herself back in her own room regarding the dark stain on her dress right between her legs.

"Oh! How could I?" she gasped. "I really enjoyed seeing it, this stain proves it. Oh! I must be going crazy. Here I am, a virgin and a pervert at the same time." She changed her dress and went out once more, meeting Mrs. Mason just coming up the stairs.

"Hello!" said Clara, trying to sound unconcerned, "I was just wondering what time dinner was served."

Mrs. Mason paused, with her hand on Clara's shoulder, as she studied her briefly. "My, but you're pretty, aren't you?" she said. "Well, if you're only hungry you won't need me." And she went on her way down the corridor, while Clara decided to explore the library until the gong might summon her to cat. Perhaps she might find some clue to what went on in the house, she thought with hazy uncertainty.

Clara had been in the library for some twenty minutes without finding a single book having a bookplate such as those in her sister's drawer, although a lot of the books were just as sexy and used the same dirty words and were all about . . . love making . . . Clara finished in her mind, although she was pretty certain that they didn't really have much to do with love.

She was bending over a low shelf, and as she rose her arm struck against a vase of flowers, and splashed it all over the dress of a woman who had been sitting reading in a chair by the window.

"I'm terribly sorry," Clara stammered, "I didn't know I was so close to your chair as that."

"Don't worry about it, my dear," the woman replied,

"it makes a woman twice as interesting if she changes her dress in the middle of the evening. Everybody suspects the worst of her. And it will only take me a minute to run upstairs and put on something else."

"Do let me come with you and help?" begged Clara, and she simply would not be refused, although the woman laughingly declared that she was quite capable of changing her own dress without the assistance of a volunteer maid.

She was a well-dressed woman in her early thirties, with gray eyes and a tip-tilted nose. She was well worth looking at, Clara decided, as she accompanied her upstairs, and she could not help wondering if she herself would remain as attractive when she reached that age. Instinctively she knew that the woman's breasts were not corseted even though they were firm and upstanding against her dress. Her step was that of a girl of twenty and her eyes were as bright and lively as a child's. Clara was curious about a woman like that. Supposing one was that age, would one's flanks and legs stay firm, or would they get flabby and would one's breasts sag?

They had reached the woman's room in the west wing of the house, and Clara entered behind her. The damp dress was put away in a cupboard, and both women stood before a mirror and admired the reflection of the elder woman's body. Her soft breasts did not pout like those of a young girl, but they had a sort of sensuous beauty that Clara envied, and the dark brown nipples were terribly attractive. The woman put lipstick on her mouth, and a tiny dab on each nipple too.

"Kissproof," she said. "It doesn't stain one's dress and the men all say that it excites them through the silk of one's blouse." She put perfume behind each ear, at the base of her neck, and touched that to her nipples too. She cast a quick sideways glance at Clara before sliding the dropper of the perfume bottle down under the band of her panties into her tiny navel and across the mound of her sex.

"If you want to help me," the woman said, "you can find a black dress for me in the closet." Clara began the search while the other was changing her shoes. "And black step-ins," the woman added, "I hate to disappoint the men."

She stood there balanced on one leg and pointing the other like a dancer, while she rolled down her discarded silk stockings. And then she turned around and Clara saw her whole nakedness for the first time. She fairly gasped at the sight of the woman standing there, adjusting her girdle, without seeming to notice the effect her nakedness was having on the girl. She stood with her youthful-seeming legs planted firmly apart, while she half turned her head to adjust a few hairs that had escaped from her careful coiffure.

The lines of her body rose in swift slopes from her full thighs to her shoulders, clean and careless. Her breasts, the nipples turned slightly away from each other, and still shining from the perfume and lipstick on them, gave to her shoulders an added solidarity, and served to balance the lovely curves of her hips, which melted from loins to thighs without a break in the perfect symmetry of her nude flesh.

But it was not only this beauty that the girl saw,

nor was it the curling dark brown hair showing between the woman's thighs, though this was what appeared to be holding Clara's gaze. In reality she was looking at a small mark on the belly several inches below the navel and just above the sex-hair, so placed that only someone who saw the woman stark naked would ever notice it.

It was a mark about the size of a half dollar, crimson as if it had been burned into the flesh. And it was, of course, in the form of a scorpion.

The woman paused in the adjustment of the black lace panties she had just donned, and frowned as she discovered that Clara was still staring at her. "Is there something wrong?" she asked. "Don't you feel well?"

"Oh! No! It isn't anything at all," Clara said, collecting her senses with great effort. "I was . . . looking at you . . . because you seem so attractive." She smiled weakly. "Do you know we don't know each other's names. I'm Clara Morrow."

"And I'm Alice Burton," the woman said. She looked at Clara with a new and pointed thoughtfulness. "Will you snap my brassiere for me, please?" she asked. She turned her naked back to the girl, and slipped her bare arms through the silk straps. Clara snapped the ends into place, and her fingers lightly touched the woman's bare shoulders as she did so, and lost in thought she let them remain there. Alice Burton stood quite still for several seconds. Then she turned and caught Clara's fingers in her hand, squeezing them in a quick and affectionate gesture. "Come here!" she said. She sat on the edge of the bed and extended one very shapely leg. She handed Clara the black silk stockings. "You can put them on me if you want to," she said.

Clara felt the strangeness of the situation but she did not understand it. She went down on one knee and embarrassedly took Mrs. Burton's small foot in her hand. She slipped on the stocking and carefully drew it up over her knee and smoothed it along the bare thigh, where she secured it with a garter. The woman extended the other leg and Clara repeated the same performance, feeling very confused at the strange sensation of holding a woman's bare leg in her hands.

"I don't . . . I'm not sure I got the seam quite straight," she apologized. "If you'll stand up for a minute I'll . . ."

Alice Burton stood up and opened her legs slightly so as to allow Clara to slip one hand between them while she adjusted the seams. Clara's face was pressed against the woman's thigh as she fumbled with her stockings, and the heavy scent of her sex and her perfume made Clara tremble with excitement.

She was trembling with a sensation of mixed attraction and repulsion which she could scarcely define to herself. "I think they're on straight now," she said.

Alice Burton put one hand on her head before she had time to get to her feet, and somehow Clara's lips brushed the other woman's thigh as she stood up. And then, before she could really stand upright, the other woman hugged her head to her thigh and sank back on the bed, with her arms firmly around the kneeling girl's shoulders.

Clara sank right back on her knees and found her face pressed unequivocally between Alice's thighs. Her

77

nostrils were choked with the sweet smell of perfume and sex, and she pulled her head away. She found Alice's eyes, bright and demanding, were dominating her. "Was I mistaken?" Alice mused.

"I don't know what you mean. I don't know what you want," Clara stammered.

"Don't you really?" Alice stroked the girl's hair. "You were looking at me as though you knew what you wanted." She raised one thigh slightly and used it to caress Clara's cheek. "But then I'm not forcing you to do anything you don't want to. You were acting as though you liked me. Really you were." Her voice lengthened suggestively on the word "liked."

Clara felt that whatever happened she must find out more about the mark on the woman's belly. Especially who had put it there. She made her decision, and turned a blushing and shamed face up to Alice's cool and questioning eyes.

"You mustn't be angry with me," she said softly. "I don't want you to be angry." She rubbed her soft face against the elder woman's thigh and smiled doubt-fully. She let her head be drawn between Alice's legs again, and her lips were gently urged to offer her a stranger kiss than anything she had ever imagined. Her mouth touched the lace fringe of the black silk panties, and she kissed first a bare hip, and then a warmly perfumed groin. Then Alice guided the girl's head deep between her thighs, and drew her lips to her crotch, offering her a kiss that was moist and odorous of sex.

"Put out your tongue," Alice whispered, bending forward. And Clara touched her tongue to the softest part of the woman's thigh, along the milk-white inner curve. Through the thin mesh of the black panties she could see the outline of the scorpion, curling his tail as though to strike down at the sex so daringly offered to him. She had been glad of the dim light before, but now she wished there was more illumination, even though it lit up her shame. Clara twined her fingers over the tops of the panties to draw them down, fastening her mind on that and not on what her mouth was destined to do.

Her lips, under the crotch of the wispy garment, found a few curling hairs that escaped from the cross strap over the cunt. And Clara's tongue dragged across the lips of the cunt itself as the cross strap slipped to one side. But suddenly, with her panties half-dragged down, Alice pushed Clara aside. "It's early yet, and we have all the evening before us," she said. She rose from the bed and recommenced dressing, leaving Clara confused and ashamed and somewhat disheveled, halfway from her knees on the floor. Rising to her feet she moved to the door.

"Where are you going?" Alice asked, catching sight of Clara's shamefaced countenance in the mirror.

"To my room," Clara answered. She lowered her eyes and added in less than a whisper, "to wash my face."

Mrs. Burton came to her side and took her by the wrist. "No, you mustn't do that," she said almost sharply. "I don't want you to wash your face, any more than I shall wash your lip rouge from my thigh. Do you understand?"

"But it makes me feel so ashamed to be this way," Clara protested.

"And that's all the more reason for staying that way. You must learn to master shame and not to fear it. Now come down and we will drink a glass of wine to our little love affair . . . and to shame," she added cynically.

And it was while they were thus toasting each other that Johnny Webster discovered them.

"I've been looking everywhere for you," he said, and he took Clara by the arm.

"But she belongs to me now," Alice Burton objected, and though at any other time the words would have seemed harmless enough, Clara crimsoned at their tone.

"Then I'll see that she comes back to you," he said as they vanished outside into the darkness.

"Where are you taking me?" Clara inquired, as they passed across the lawn.

"To meet two friends of mine." He guided her into the shadow of an arbor with a swing seat in it.

"You were gone a long time," a girl's voice said out of the shadows. Clara could just see two dim figures on a low wall at one side of the arbor.

"I had a hard time finding her," Webster said.

"We almost didn't wait," the girl said. "Just look what happened." And then Clara realized that the girl was lying on the wall, naked as the day she was born, her clothes a rumpled heap beside her. She was half in the man's arms, and Clara saw that she had his trousers open and was holding his throbbing prick in her hand.

Clara turned away in embarrassment, but Johnny's grip on her arm tightened. "Oh, please take me back to the house," she pleaded as she tried to wrench her arm free from his grasp.

"I told you she was a virgin," Johnny told the others in triumphant tones. "But all the same she'll do what I tell her to and like it!" And in Clara's ear he whispered, "Unless you do just what I tell you, and without any nonsense, I'll take off all your clothes and march you back to the house that way . . . to Mrs. Mason."

He felt her wilt a little at that and seized his chance, taking her suddenly in his arms, his hands slipping into her dress and over her breasts. "So you'll do as I say," he told her quietly. And she, looking over his shoulder at the smiling and naked girl and the man on the low wall, whispered hopelessly . . . "Oh! Yes . . ."

She felt him lifting her dress and she did not try to stop him. He raised it over her hips, and then he turned her body toward him and let the other two watch her face while he pulled her dress still higher, and then dragged down her panties from her loins and buttocks. She stood there with him, trying to keep her face hidden in his shoulder, while her legs grew weaker and more and more trembly.

"Not with them here," she pleaded. "Take me somewhere else if you must have me." It seemed so terrible that he should let other people watch . . . monstrous that they should see him pluck the clothes from her shrinking body. Everything in that dark arbor was somehow happening in a strange, unreal world. The naked girl on the wall, saying something in a soft, distant voice, was unreal too, as unreal as she herself, Clara, had now become. It could not be she whose bare behind was so scandalously on display, not she who quivered before another man's eyes as Johnny passed his fingers down the groove of her ass, and it certainly could not be she who was now standing there with a man's erect prick pulsing in her hand.

"Now take off all your clothes and let us see you naked!" Johnny ordered, as he removed his tantalizing hand from where it had been plucking at her furry mount.

She did not want to cry. She did not even feel like crying. But she was crying as she whispered, "Oh! No!" and as she said it began to obey. She took off her dress, not daring to look at the two who were watching her, and then she took off her shoes and stockings. Her panties were held up by just one big button at the side, and Johnny had unfastened that. She had been keeping them up by pressing outwards with her knees, and now she relaxed and let them slip down to her feet. Her brassiere went too, as Johnny made an impatient movement.

She stood there in her bashful nakedness, the flagging under her bare feet feeling damp and cool, and she clutched herself tightly under the arms and across her shrinking rosy breasts. She felt the three of them watching her, and she kept her eyes fixed on her pink toes. Webster touched her knee, and then his hand closed on her thigh. He pulled her hands away from her own body and made her turn round, while he smoothed his own hands over her dimpled back and across the crease of her buttocks. Again he put her hand on his prick, which was thrusting rampantly from his trousers, making her hold it in her slim fingers and squeeze it gently.

"Now rub it between your legs," he said. Clara held his cock against her own hairiness, firmly in her reluctant crotch. She squeezed her thighs together and rubbed his warm and quite unyielding sex with them and with her hands. "No! Open your lips and rub it in your cunt," Johnny said. And so she pressed the throbbing weapon between the dry lips of her slit. She had to stand on her toes to do it, because of the difference in their heights, and so she leaned upon him, rocking back and forth as she rubbed herself against him. Her cunt grew wet from his own spend, and then it began to feel nice and she grew even wetter as her own juice welled out.

Johnny was feeling her breasts and her behind, bruising her nipples with the roughness of his jacket as he pressed her against him. He felt all of her nakedness there in the darkness that was still not dark enough . . . and where his fingers caressed her body she could still feel them there afterwards. She was on fire with shame and excitement, and his fingers left little cold thrills up and down her body.

"You tickle so!" she said, and was surprised to hear her own voice add in a little laugh of its own volition, a little laugh that she had certainly neither intended nor expected.

He made her kneel on her rumpled pile of clothes, and he stood there close in front of her. He took her hands and made her caress his cock. It was moist and smelled of her own cunt, and it slipped in her slim fingers. He squeezed her hands around it and rubbed it between their palms. She did not feel the night's coolness at all. Her body was burning. So was her face.

The wind played with her hair and flung it over her face and across his balls, and she was glad of the momentary eclipse.

Clara felt that the night had fingers, that it touched her too, and toyed with her bare body. Pride was gone, and all that had been part of her pride in herself was gone too. People were watching her do this. She felt nothing but shame, was aware of nothing but shame. Her momentary excitement when she rubbed his prick inside the petals of her cunt was gone. She was shamed in her own eyes, shamed before Webster, shamed before the two strangers on the wall.

Here in the dark her shame grew and grew until her whole body burned with it. Her erect nipples felt the sharp caress of the avid male who stood before her, and suddenly she realized that he was not really touching them. It was shame that plucked at them and that passed mocking fingers all over her naked body. No tears, she reflected, would ever wash that stain away.

Johnny's voice came back to her. "Suck it," he demanded, "take it in your mouth and suck it." He thrust his prick right in her face, and pulled her head toward his crotch. "Kiss and suck it!" he said harshly.

Clara put her tongue out, knowing that the man and woman on the wall had leaned forward to defeat the darkness which did not cloak her abasement. She found his organ with the tip of her tongue, and her lips quivered. A sharp taste, which she realized must be that of her own sex, made her mouth suddenly wet. She ran her tongue slowly up and down, making his prick sway stiffly. Then her fingers curved underneath it and she clasped it to her mouth, caressing the sides and the red tip. She held it up and licked beneath it, up and down the channel where the rim of the head came together in the little slotted hole at the tip, licking him all the way down to his balls. His hands were buried in her hair, holding her fiercely to her task.

Suddenly the other girl sprang down from the wall and knelt beside Clara. She felt a soft naked thigh touch hers as the girl went down on the cool flagging too. A quick hand was slipped over Clara's as she held Johnny's prick, and the soft voice of the other girl whispered in her ear, "Lick it with me, darling." The girl was facing Clara now, with her cheek up against the man's thigh, and her lips pressing through the matted hair around his sex. Then they touched Clara's, kissing her warm lips over the arched prick which moistened them. Her tongue touched Clara's mouth, then the throbbing prick, then Clara's lips once more.

"Lick it with me, darling!" the girl repeated, but this time not in any whisper. Her mouth pressed upon Johnny's cock, squeezing it down upon Clara's mouth, and she caressed it with her tongue. She put one arm round Clara, holding her breast in one hand, and their near breasts touched, their nipples rubbing together. Then her hand slipped down over Clara's buttocks and between her legs in a more insistent caress.

Then she tried to push the head of the man's prick into Clara's mouth, but Clara wouldn't accept it. She slipped her lips away and slid her tongue under the head of the prick that thrust toward her lips. On the other side she felt the girl's tongue slide over hers and pause to caress it. She curled her tongue in another direction, but the girl's tongue was there too, this time

85

pressing under hers and partly into her mouth. She let the girl take her tongue and suck it, allowing it to slip into the groove that the other girl expertly made in the curled up length of her own tongue.

The girl completely dominated her, finally urging her until she was caressing Johnny's balls with her lips, nuzzling at their elastic curves. Though they were both subservient to the man, their subjugation was not equal, for Clara was subject to the girl as well. The wantonness of this girl seemed to have no bounds. By now she was taking Johnny's balls in her mouth, singly and together, and sucking them tenderly. And suddenly she took the spongy tip of his prick in her mouth and began to suck it. And as she sucked, her open lips met and caressed Clara's.

She tried to pull away, but before she realized it her tongue was sucked into the girl's mouth too. Her caressing lips pressed the man's penis and Clara's tongue together. Clara's tongue-tip was curled over the bud of the head until she did manage to jerk her head away.

The other girl's mouth released its captive with an audible "pop." She looked questioningly at Clara. "Do you want to suck it by yourself?" she queried.

Clara's "No!" was more of a sob than an answer, and she would have twisted her head away if Webster and the girl had not been holding her too tightly. "Then go on licking it while I suck it," the girl exclaimed. She waited until she saw that Clara was going to obey her, and then she slipped the prick back into her own mouth. She put her hand between his thighs and tickled his balls lovingly. Clara felt that she would be smothered in the close embrace, but she continued to caress the man's sex as well as she could with the tip and blade of her tongue Her unwillingly willing obedience surprised her.

Suddenly the other girl's slender naked body was jerking in a convulsive effort. The man's buttocks were quivering and his hips jerked frantically back and forth. Clara was quite bewildered for a moment, and then she realized that Johnny had spent, and that the girl had swallowed it and was sucking for more. She felt that she could not bear it, and she closed her eyes to shut out the sight of the tall O of the girl's mouth where the prick disappeared into it.

Webster suddenly pushed both their heads away and then stepped back. With her eyes closed Clara could hear the other girl pantingly catch her breath. She could not bear to look at her. And then the swelling prick was thrust against her lips once more. She returned to caressing it almost without thinking and she felt the other girl's mouth contact hers as it pressed down again, touching her tongue. She kept her eyes tightly shut and went on with her task.

And then after a few moments she realized that it could not be Johnny who was standing over her. A new man-scent was coming to her nostrils, and she looked up to find that the other man was leaning down to watch her over his prick, on which she was lavishing such ardent caresses. When he saw that she was trying to escape he tightened his knees on her white shoulders, while the girl also clutched her by the arm.

"You're not going to stop now, after such a promising start, are you?" said the man in a deep voice.

"I didn't realize . . ." cried Clara incoherently. "Both

87

of you . . . two . . . I don't . . . please let me go."

"It isn't any worse to do it with one than with the other," said the girl dispassionately. "You didn't even know the difference between them till you opened your eyes."

Clara turned to Johnny, who was still sitting on the wall and watching the proceedings with interest. "Take me away," she begged him, "you can do what you like with me after, only take me away from here."

"When you've finished what you started," he told her, with a grin. "This is hardly the time to become choosy. You've already had one man, and I can't see why you object to a change. Don't they all taste pretty much alike?" he added, addressing the other girl.

"Practically," the girl laughed back. "Make her suck it if she doesn't want to lick it. Maybe it would be fun to see your virgin girlfriend suck off my husband? Darling, tell me, did you ever have a virgin suck you off?"

Clara glanced at the other girl's sticky mouth and tried not to remember what she had seen her do. The girl rubbed at Clara's mouth with the end of her husband's prick and whispered in her ear. Clara flushed hotly. "No! I won't say such a lie!" she flared hotly back.

"Say it, or I'll make you suck him off, and swallow it when he comes as well," the girl insisted, pressing Clara's head down to her repugnant task.

So poor Clara said it as softly as she could, but they could all hear her shamed voice whisper, "I liked licking it!" And she began licking the big prick again, while the man sat back to enjoy himself. Clara's tongue was sore by this time and she began to use her lips more, running her mouth up and down his rampant sex, but never allowing the tip to go into her own mouth. Some people have prejudices, and this was hers.

She helped the other girl in her caresses by holding the prick in her hands while she mouthed up and down to the tip, finally lipping the tip too. "It's no worse than doing it to Johnny," she kept telling herself, but then she remembered that yesterday she had thought that was awful too, so she stopped thinking and just set herself to doing what her tormentors wanted.

At length the jerking motions of the man's hips and his heavy breathing told the girl that he was approaching the crisis so she pushed Clara to one side and took the whole of his sex in her own mouth. This time Clara saw exactly what happened. She saw the girl sucking frantically and driving her mouth up and down and shaking her head from side to side in a perfect frenzy. Her eyes closed in ecstasy and then fluttered wildly as her husband came. She swallowed deliriously for a moment, and then it was all over, and the man's sex came out of his wife's mouth soft and dripping.

The other girl got to her feet, but Clara stayed there kneeling until Johnny touched her on the shoulder. Then she too stood up, and he held her panties for her to step into, and hooked her brassiere for her. Now that it was all over she hurried on her clothes as quickly as possible, so as to avoid any further contact with the other two witnesses to her shame, and seeking out the darkest shadows on the way, she returned alone to the house.

Chapter 7

"Where have you been?" said Mrs. Burton, as Clara entered the hall. "I've been looking for you everywhere."

"I feel very tired," Clara said. "I'd rather not talk now if you don't mind."

"Do you want me to take you back to your room?" Alice put her arm around Clara's waist and put her hand gently on her behind. Then her hand moved around to the waist and pressed her belly softly. In her mind's eye Clara suddenly saw the mark of the scorpion on the woman's belly in almost exactly the same spot.

"Yes, please," she said, and they went upstairs together.

When Clara had closed and locked the door of her room she turned around and saw that Alice had entered behind her and was watching her. She said nothing, but went over to the window casement and looked out over the lawn, wondering if she should close this too.

Alice came across the room and stood beside her. "Do you find the country lonesome?" she inquired. Her fingers touched Clara's arms and slipped down, more curiously than amorously, to caress her breasts and soothe them.

"I like it," Clara answered suddenly.

"Do you?" Alice asked softly. "Do you really?" She put her hand out and squeezed one of Clara's breasts harder, feeling for the nipple, while her other hand went down between her thighs and took hold of Clara's pussy with a rolling caress.

"Yes, I like it," Clara said. She let herself lean back against the woman, feeling her knees against the back of her own, feeling the warmth of the woman's belly against her own bottom. Alice turned to one side to rub her thigh against Clara and that reminded Clara that the mark of her lips was still in the same place.

Alice let down the Venetian blind, and led Clara away from the window, snapping out all but one small lamp . . . the one farthest from the bed. "Take off your dress, and I'll take off mine," she said softly. "After that we can undress each other."

For a moment Clara wanted to run from the room. She watched Alice take off her dress, and she stood for several moments with clenched hands while Alice stood there in her own undies waiting for Clara to undress. Finally she forced herself to commence what was expected of her, though she felt that she could really bear no more tonight, even if it were to be of a pleasant nature. Standing before the mirror where she could watch every gesture, she quickly loosened her dress and slipped it off over her head. Her brassiere was twisted where she had hurriedly put it on in the arbor.

"Come to bed!" said Alice. She sat as she had done once before, on the edge of the bed, and wordlessly told Clara to kneel. She extended her shapely legs while the young girl took off her shoes. She rested her silk-clad foot on the girl's thigh and held up the other for the stocking to be stripped off the dainty limb. Clara tried not to feel the sensual softness of the thighs she touched. "Now my brassiere," said the woman, and Clara leaned close between the soft, spreading legs and embraced her body so as to reach around for the straps.

Alice hugged her with her legs, leaning back on her arms as she did so, but on realizing Clara's embarrassment she put out a lazy hand and wantonly disordered Clara's dark hair with her errant fingers. Then she leaned back once more on stiff arms, and raised her fanny while Clara stripped down the black silk panties.

Clara stared at the scorpion on the woman's belly, and while she looked at it the curled tail seemed to writhe. She touched it, and found the skin scarred but soft to touch. "What is that?" she asked, as if she had only just noticed it.

"One of my lovers put it there, but we won't talk about it now, perhaps later," replied Alice, and Clara realized that it was a topic requiring delicate approach. "Do you see where you kissed me?" said Alice, pointing to a reddish mark on her thigh. "Have your thighs ever had lipstick on them?" she added.

"I've never . . . been with a woman," said Clara bashfully. Alice was holding the tips of Clara's fingers on the mossy hair which only half concealed her slit, and Clara's whole hand felt prickly. She realized that she was on the brink of experiences which were totally new to her, and her thoughts were swinging wildly from hope to fear and then back again.

Suddenly Alice stood up. "Now it's my turn to undress you!" she said softly. She made Clara take her place on the bed while she knelt and took off her shoes and stockings. She took a much longer time over it than Clara had, pausing quite often to stroke and feel the girl's legs and thighs and play with the dark hair curling over her slit. Next she removed Clara's brassiere, leaning far forward and nipping at her breasts with her lips as she did so. Clara was a little bit surprised and shocked for a moment, but nothing more happened just then.

Next Alice pulled her panties down. "Let me see all of you," she said. "Keep your legs apart. Good and wide." She thrust her fingers boldly into Clara's crotch and caressed her cunt. Clara squirmed and wanted to cover herself with her two hands. Alice tickled her cunt once more just lightly, and then leaned forward and seized her breasts as they jutted out in all their lovely nakedness, with the lamplight shining on them. "Perhaps we'd better get into bed," she said, and made Clara climb under the covers with her.

Enfolded in a warm embrace, Clara shivered as though she was chilled. Alice's hands slid down her back and over her flanks. They passed slowly over her belly and closed on her twin breasts, shaking them briskly for a moment or two until Clara was lulled peacefully by the sensation and was almost sorry when she stopped.

Then Alice showed the younger girl how to rub nipples, touching the plum-like points of her own breasts to the pink tips of Clara's lovely mounds, until they became hard and even stung a little. She drew Clara closely to her and their bare bellies rubbed together and the hair of their pussies tangled as one of Alice's thighs began to force its way between hers. Petting her, pinching her buttocks, kissing her full upon the mouth whenever an objection seemed imminent, Alice slid one thigh into Clara's crotch and moved it up and down there in a sensuous rhythm.

"You're afraid of me, aren't you?" she asked Clara, taking her caressing tongue out of Clara's warm mouth long enough to ask and receive an answer.

"Why should I be afraid of you?" Clara countered in a voice that trembled in spite of herself. Alice wriggled nearer, pressing her thigh heavily on Clara's cunt, sliding it up and down in the growing wetness that began to form between the spread lips as they flattened out on the pressing leg.

"Take my breasts in your hands if you're not afraid of me," she said. "Do the things that I do!"

Clara took hold of the woman's breasts. They were much softer than hers . . . maturity had done that . . . and when she closed her palms on them they crushed like tender blossoms. Soon Alice sighed and gripped Clara's thigh with both her own, rubbing her cunt slipperily up and down on Clara's slim leg, while she pressed her own thigh up between Clara's and against her cunt. Clara's head began to swim. She wished her cunt wasn't so wet . . . it seemed awful to be so excited by things like this, but she noticed with a subconscious thrill of pride that her slit was almost as wet as the other woman's.

"Put your other hand on my bottom," Alice said. "Put your finger down in the crease." Clara slid her hand over the round buttocks and then squeezed them, passing her finger up deeply into the crease. "Oh! My darling!" Alice exclaimed, "you have your finger in my cunt!" Clara had no time to be surprised by this denouement, for Alice rolled her over onto her back and pressed her delta into Clara's crotch. Hair was tickling the girl's cunt, and she felt the warm lips of the other cunt rubbing against hers.

For a moment she wondered how such a result had been achieved, and began to pull her fingers out from her friend's bottom. "No, keep your finger in me," Alice cried, reaching behind her and holding Clara to her previous task. She moved her hips as a man would have had he been fucking a girl, and the front of her slit and the girl's touched at the clitoris, while Clara's finger lost itself in the warm grasp of the woman's actual hole.

Then Alice began to kiss and suck the young girl's pink nipples, and each time she pulled on them with her lips Clara could feel the thrill right deep down in her cunt. The keen pleasure was mounting in her body more and more sharply, and she whispered, "Don't stop!" Alice didn't stop, and suddenly a spasm spread through her whole body, thrill after thrill, and she lay with her legs wide apart and her cunt dripping wet with love juice as she pressed her taut breasts fiercely against Alice's plucking lips.

Alice slipped off her and lay on her back, with her

own legs open and a trickle of love juice running down them. "Oh! Darling!" she exclaimed, "fuck me the way I fucked you. Ohh! Come on, child, love me!" She plunged her hand between Clara's thighs, rubbing the dainty lips of her slit together.

"I'm ashamed to!" Clara pleaded. "It seems such a dirty thing to do!"

"Then be ashamed, if you must," replied Alice. "But fuck me the way Johnny Webster fucked you tonight!" She rubbed her crotch against Clara's and pushed her finger deep into her yielding sex.

"He didn't," cried Clara, "he didn't do any such thing."

"Then tell me what he did do," said the woman. "Didn't he put his prick where my finger is now? And didn't he rub it in and out like this? And didn't you like it?"

"I won't tell you what he did," Clara exclaimed. Then she remembered something, and she went on, "Unless you tell me who put that scorpion mark on your belly."

Alice Burton squeezed the girl closer in her arms. "I am certain we have sufficient pleasant occupations for tonight without telling each other stories. Suck my breasts and fuck me hard, Clara darling."

Clara put her mouth down to the woman's breasts and began to caress her nipples with her lips. Then she commenced to lick them, and then, as Alice had done, she began to suck. She moved her hips too, and rubbed her open cunt with the curly hair of her own crotch. She began to do it quite hard. She would not have admitted it for the world, but she rather liked the strange feeling, and Alice's finger in her moist cunt was exciting her terribly.

"Clara," the woman said suddenly, "what was it that he made you do? Johnny, I mean. It was something you had to be on your knees for, and with all your clothes off. What was it?" She closed her soft thighs on Clara's and rubbed her moist cunt on the girl's leg. Then she pressed Clara's yielding body back onto the bed, and stroked her sex with her slender fingers in a hundred delectable ways that would have overcome the reticence of a saint. Clara let her thighs spread farther and farther apart. Of her own accord she took one of the woman's nipples with her tongue and lips as the white bosom brushed her cheek.

"He made me . . . made me lick it . . . his prick," she blurted out. She did not say what else she had had to do in the arbor.

"And he didn't fuck you or make you suck him off?" Alice coaxed softly. Clara shook her head in denial. "Would you like to kiss my cunt tonight?" the woman went on. "Would you, Clara darling? Shall we lie here and kiss each other like that?" She kissed the insides of Clara's white thighs, brushing her pussy with her cheek as she did so.

A shudder that was purely involuntary ran through Clara's body at the sensual contact. "Don't make me," she pleaded, "I don't want anyone's sex tonight. I'm too tired."

"But you won't be angry if I do it to you, will you?" And Alice kissed her deeply between her thighs, pressing her mouth to the moist and flowering cunt with no more concern than if it had been a lover's lips that she caressed.

"You've done this to a lot of girls, haven't you?" asked Clara, fascinated as she watched Alice's tongue reaching and curling, slender and pink between her thighs.

"That's not a fair question," laughed Alice, "and it's a foolish one too." She nestled her head down between Clara's legs and kissed her sex hotly, and for the first time in her modest sexual experience Clara felt a sense of superiority and a kind of domination. And that it should be an older and more experienced woman who was in the inferior position made the sensation doubly gratifying. She began to feel a real and thrilling sexual delight and a terrible urge to carry the situation further.

"How long ago was it that you first kissed a girl's cunt?" Clara demanded, her voice strangely triumphant and her hips quivering with excitement.

"A girl's cunt? Oh, long ago. I was younger than you are," replied Alice, as she gently squeezed Clara's breasts in her two hands until the nipples pouted and hardened like two ripe cherries.

"And then that mark on your belly was burned there to make you feel ashamed, wasn't it?" Clara asked with sudden insight. "And that's why you let it be put there, wasn't it, so that any time a man saw you all naked he'd know what . . . what . . ."

"What a bitch I was, what a sweet hot dirty bitch! But don't let us talk about it." And as she spoke Alice ran her tongue over Clara's slit and then thrust deeply into it. Clara's breath came through her teeth violently.

She looked down between her breasts and over the mount at the woman's head where it shook from side to side as it pressed against her cunt and sucked eagerly at the yielding lips. Clara laughed out loud. "Rub right inside my cunt with your tongue," she ordered. It was the first sexual demand she had ever made, and it thrilled her deep down inside.

Alice obeyed, just as though it were natural for the one who was being sucked to say where she wanted it. And Clara laughed again. "Now I'm going to put my finger in your cunt just as deep as you put your tongue in mine," she added.

"No, use your thumb," the woman gasped, and Clara prodded the wetly open sex with her thumb, while the questing tongue in her own cunt excited her more and more.

"Ohh! Ohh! Stop . . . please stop!" she cried suddenly. "No more! Oh, stop!" But Alice did not stop. Clara's breath was now coming in gasps and her flanks were trembling violently. Her head was reeling. "Oh God! You must stop!" she cried. "I can't stand any more!"

But now more violently than ever the woman's lips were sucking and pressing on Clara's cunt, while her thighs were held apart by roughly caressing fingers. Clara could see Alice's sex as through a mist. It had become very red where she had been rubbing it, and it was as wet as a garden after a storm. It did not close tightly on her thumb any more. It was wide open, and her thumb and forefinger together drove forward into a deep pink hole. Suddenly she felt the same thing happen to her. "Alice has raped me," she thought, as a probing finger was thrust through the virgin opening, plunging and turning almost roughly.

Clara almost fainted at the lovely sensation, but even that was not the end, for a moment later another finger, wetted in Clara's own love juice, penetrated insinuatingly into her behind, stopping just inside and shaking the yielding flesh without slipping in and out. Clara was shaken with sobs of ecstasy. Her whole body quivered with emotion. She squirmed in frenzy, and suddenly she discovered that the other woman's slit was much closer to her than before. Alice had twisted her body around till the parted lips of her slit were only inches from Clara's mouth.

"I . . . I . . . Ohhh!" Clara expostulated weakly. Then she was silent, for her mouth had been forced by the jerking of her own body to touch the lips of her companion's cunt. The taste was salt but after all not unpleasant, she decided. Her fingers opened the pink folds still wider, and her tongue hesitatingly licked at the flowing juice. Then she began to suck at it more eagerly, frantically, her mouth and her lips moving more and more rapidly and in unison.

Alice enveloped her whole sex with her caressing mouth, and roughly tongued the protruding clitoris. Clara moaned with pleasure as her sexy impulses grew and grew. Playing with her own body over her sister's smutty books had never brought a thrill like this. All her muscles tightened in an ecstatic impulse as she came, and she would have screamed aloud with her delight but for the hot wet sex that covered her mouth. So she thrust her tongue deep within it instead, and spent quiveringly again and again. . . .

Chapter 8

Clara drove into the city next day with Mrs. Mason, and hurried straight to the D.A.'s office.

"If it's a man friend you're so eager to meet you can invite him to come back with you on a visit," said Mrs. Mason as they parted. "If you like him so much I'm sure I should be delighted to meet him one weekend."

The secretary ushered Clara straight into Conrad's office when she arrived. "I'd begun to worry about you," he told her as she sat down. "I was expecting you to phone."

"I wouldn't have dared to tell you over the phone," she replied. "You'd never believe what I found out."

"First," he said, drawing his chair nearer and patting her knee as he did so, "how much did your information cost you to acquire it?" Clara blushed scarlet, and Conrad raised his eyebrows quizzically. "That much, eh! Well, we'll discuss that later. What did you find out?"

"To begin with, it's an amazing place," said Clara. "Quite crazy really and full of weird people. You're invited to come back with me on a visit. Everybody seems to be there for just one purpose . . . to go to bed with everybody else. It's terrible to think of, but that's where Rita must have been all those times when I didn't know where she was."

"Did you find any trace of her?" demanded Conrad.

"No, not exactly. But I saw a cat-of-nine-tails just like the one we found in her drawer. And I discovered that one of the women there had a mark burned on her stomach. A red scorpion!"

The D.A. passed his hand over his face. "I don't know what to say. Are you sure it wasn't some sort of birthmark?"

"Oh! No!" said Clara quickly. "I examined it closely, it was burned right in. . . ." She hesitated a moment. "I don't know what you'll think of me," she continued, biting her lips, "but I couldn't help what happened. I . . . I had to find out. First this Webster man I told you about . . . he guessed I was there spying . . . and he threatened to tell Mrs. Mason unless I . . ."

"Unless you were willing to make certain concessions to him?" Conrad interrupted.

"Yes! That's right!" Clara hesitated. "He made me do awful things." And she told him. Everything. Webster and the man and girl in the arbor in the garden, Alice Burton, and the pair in the big bedroom with the mirrors and the whipping . . . and when she had finished she felt as if she had experienced it herself all over again. When she had concluded her story she waited, but Conrad made no comment. She tried to guess from his face what he might be thinking, but she could tell nothing.

"We'll go over it more thoroughly at your house tonight," he said as she left. "Look over that diary again before I get there, the whole key to the story may be in it. . . ."

"Do you want to look at the things here?" Clara asked, as she and the D.A. paused for a moment in the hall on his arrival.

"No, don't bother to bring the drawer down here, we can look at them just as well upstairs, the way we did before," he replied.

So Clara led him upstairs to her sister's bedroom and unlocked the bureau drawer. The D.A. took out the cat-of-nine-tails and dangled the light leather straps in his hand. "You say this is like the one you saw in the house?" he inquired.

"Well, almost, but not quite as heavy . . . this one . . . I mean."

He examined the lash. "It's very well made," he admitted. "A soft enough leather so that it won't cut the skin, but still heavy enough to sting quite a bit. I wonder how intimate Rita was with it?" He picked up the diary from the drawer and ran through it. "This seems to be what I was looking for," he said, "will you read it for me?"

Clara looked at him doubtfully, but she took the diary and sat down on the bed beside him, with one leg drawn up under her. She began to read in a voice which at first was hesitant but then grew stronger:

"Frank was very angry when I told him why I was late, and said that I deserved to be punished. Next time, he told me, I would be sure to remember that I had an appointment. Then he told me to take off all my clothes, and I did. He sent me to the closet to bring him the whip that he kept there, and when he took it and swished it through the air all its tails whistled sharply. I imagined it whistling like that over my naked bottom and I began to feel hot all over. He told me to go into the next room, and as he followed me he switched my thighs and legs once or twice from behind, not hard but enough to make me dance and become anxious for him to use it in real earnest.

"There was a very large armchair in the room, and he pointed to it with the whip. 'Stand on that and bend over the back,' he ordered, and in a moment there I was with my head hanging down toward the floor and my bottom up in the air and as tight as a drum that is waiting to be beaten. My legs were spread apart so as to steady me, and I was sure that he must be able to see my sex quite plainly by the back entrance.

"I could hear him behind me swishing the whip, and the sound excited me so that I could hardly keep still. He saw this and began to tease me. First he laid the whip on my bare behind, and slowly drew it away so that the thin leather slithered over my thighs. I waited for him to begin, but the moments passed and nothing happened. I could bear it no longer, and I lifted my head and begged him to start.

"I was ready to go on my knees to him and plead that he whip me when the lash fell. The thongs stung sweetly across my bare behind. Next time he struck harder and my bottom stung so excitingly. Soon there was not a spot that the whip had missed, but still he did not touch my bare back or legs, although he had been beating me for several minutes. My behind was pink all over by this time. But he seemed to know just when I was as hot as whipping alone could make me, and he helped me down from the chair and made me bend over one of its arms.

"I could feel him caressing my burning bottom and gently parting my thighs, and then his prick was touching the lips of my cunt. 'Just once or twice to tickle you and make you open up properly,' he said. And in another minute he was right up me to his balls, his prick slipping in and out through a flood of love juice caused by my whipping. It was so thrilling I almost fainted."

"That's enough," said Conrad. He glanced down at Clara's rounded knee as he took the diary from her. With a flippant gesture he used the whip in his hand to raise her skirt far up enough to disclose all the length of her bare thighs.

"I wonder if this is the whip he used?" he mused, as he flicked Clara's leg with it lightly. "Well, we'll never know until we find Rita," he concluded. He leaned forward and slid his hand under Clara's dress, caressing her bare leg. "Do you know," he said, "that when I look at you I simply can't believe that you did all the things you told me about."

Clara looked down at her hands, which she kept folded in her lap, and he began to stroke and pinch her more than attractive behind. "Perhaps what you need is for me to use this whip on your bottom," he suggested. He pulled her around on the bed with him, his hand still wandering under her dress and much higher up than before. He used his other hand to unzip his fly, and then he suddenly leaned over Clara, pulling her dress right up and pressing his sex against her bare thigh.

"You need either a whipping or a fucking!" he said, "and perhaps both." He pulled her pink panties down and slid his hand across her delta, his fingertips just touching the thin slit of her cunt. He rubbed his prick up along her leg, and then lay on top of her, thrusting it between her thighs.

Clara was still trying to find an answer to what he had said to her. "Don't talk like that to me," she finally said in a whisper. "You know I couldn't help what I did."

Conrad released her from his embrace and with gentle fingers began to take off her clothes. When she was naked he pushed her to the floor, making her kneel between his legs. "Do you swear to me that you haven't been fucked?" he queried.

"Ohh! You know I wasn't," she cried indignantly.

"Then show me what Webster and the other man made you do!" he demanded.

"But why?" pleaded Clara.

"Because I tell you to," he ordered. Now he abandoned the pretense of using this investigation to find Rita. "Unless you show me just what you did with them I'll give you a good spanking and a fucking as well." He took her hands and placed his prick between them. "He made you hold him this way," he said. "Then what did you do?"

Clara held herself away from him, but Conrad pulled at her head insistently, and suddenly she capitulated and began to kiss his prick. "And while you were doing that the other girl was sucking his cock?" he queried, watching Clara's face as she blushed with embarrassment at the recollection of what had occurred.

"She was sucking my tongue with it, she was awfully dirty!" Clara stammered. "She threatened to make me do it too if I wouldn't go on and lick her husband . . . after Johnny had . . . was . . . finished!"

"But how could she have made you do that?" Conrad asked her skeptically.

"She and her husband were both holding my head. Then she took his prick . . . and put it against my mouth in front . . . like this. . . ."

"Are you sure it wasn't like this?" Conrad demanded. He moved quickly and Clara suddenly found the head of his cock in her mouth and his hand behind her neck preventing her from pulling away. His lip curled at his easy success. He slid his cock a little further into Clara's mouth, rubbed it gently on the wet warmth of her tongue, and then took it out.

She crumpled into a small naked heap at his feet, the back of her hand flung across her mouth. Her eyes were two pools of disillusion. Suddenly she saw the scene in which she was playing a part . . . a naked girl sitting on the floor between a man's legs, the lights full on, and he fully dressed while she held his prick in her mouth. She just caught herself from fainting. Conrad was speaking.

"See how easy it would be for me to make you sit and suck me off," he said, thrusting his words against her silence, "but I don't want to do that . . . yet, though you will when I tell you to."

Clara shook her head mutely and closed her eyes. She hardly realized what he was talking about, and was almost glad to return to some familiar experience, obeying his hands when they gently urged her head up to lick his prick again. She did it thoroughly and wetly, practically taking it in her mouth more than once. Conrad wondered why she made such a point of not sucking him when she seemed willing to do everything else. Women were curious beings, he decided. After a few minutes he made her stop.

"Now hold it at the base of your neck, so that my balls are between your breasts," he told her. "No, keep on caressing it with your hand!" So Clara pressed the tip into the hollow of her throat and felt the swing of his balls in between her breasts as she caressed his shaft with her slim fingers. In a few minutes his prick jerked frantically and he spent, the sperm pulsing in great jets all over her throat and bosom, and trickling down over her shoulders, until Conrad sat up and wiped it off with the tangled strands of her dark hair.

If she had loved him, it would have been a beautiful thing for her to do, she felt, but as it was it only seemed simply wanton and degrading. She was horrified that she could have considered it so dispassionately at such a moment.

"You do it too well," Conrad was saying, "and much too enthusiastically for a girl who has only done it three or four times in her life." He rubbed his softened sex across her lips and the salt taste of his sperm startled her. "It won't kill you," he mocked, as she wiped her tongue on the back of her hand.

"Now put on your clothes. We have an appointment with your Mrs. Mason, and we mustn't keep her waiting too long."

He toyed with the whip while she bent over to pick up her panties, and touched her sharply on her bare buttocks with the stinging thong. "The Scorpion's sting," he suggested, as he watched the pink streaks spread and disappear on the young girl's sensitive behind.

Clara, turning to a mirror to fix her hair, stared at the sensual curl on her lips, as her flushed face regarded her from the glass, and wondered if she would like to feel the lash curl around her naked thighs in real earnest. It would depend on who did it, she decided, and found herself blushing scarlet at the thought.

Chapter 9

"*I* like your view better than mine," Conrad said, as he looked out of Clara's bedroom window.

Clara glanced up at him. "Oh! Yes!" she said with a tiny chuckle, "I suppose Mrs. Mason gives the girls the rooms with the best views on the theory that the men will spend most of their time in them as well." She put her lipstick away, and they left the room together.

As they passed down the hall he touched Clara's arm in a gesture of surprise. "That was queer," he said, "did you see it?"

"No, what?" said Clara.

"A girl came out of that corner room looking as if she was just leaving heaven. The door shut behind her quickly and she went dashing off down the corridor."

"I don't suppose it was anything," said Clara, "just your imagination."

"Don't be so foolish," replied Conrad. "It was really very peculiar. Besides . . . look at that."

Another girl was tapping lightly on the door he had indicated, glancing around idly as she waited for an answer. Conrad and Clara stepped back and peeped at her around a corner. The door opened in a moment and she slipped in.

"That really was rather odd," said Clara, "I wonder what can be going on in there?"

"That," said the D.A. emphatically, "is what we shall find out if we sit on this chest in the corner and wait."

Time passed slowly. "I don't think she's coming out again," Clara said finally, "I guess it was just an ordinary sex affair. No! Wait! Did you hear something? A sort of scuffle and a girl's voice?"

"I thought I did," said Conrad, cocking his ear, "yes, there it is again. See if you can make it out."

Clara strained her ears as the sounds grew louder but still indistinguishable. Nothing could be deduced from them. "Ah! Another caller," said Conrad softly. A red-headed girl passed them without a second glance, knocked softly on the door, and went in.

"Well, it might be anything," admitted Clara. "Only . . . what? Listen. There's that noise again. How very odd."

"Whatever it is," said the D.A., "we ought to know about it. But how? That's the question."

"I could find out what it is," said Clara suddenly. "I just bet I could."

She grabbed Conrad by the hand and pulled him back into her room. "Don't go away," she said, "I'll be back in a few minutes with the information."

"But it may be dangerous . . ." he objected, "I think I'd better . . ."

"No! You wait here." She shook her head at him and left quickly.

It was half an hour by the D.A.'s watch when she came back. "Whatever happened?" he demanded, as he saw her.

Clara leaned against the door when she had closed it. Her make-up was smeared from crying, and her

111

clothing was all disordered. The pins were gone from her hair and her eyes were red from the tears which still ran down her face.

"They whipped me!" she sobbed. "They whipped me! They took off all my clothes and whipped me!" She threw herself face down on the bed, clutching a pillow to her breasts and sobbing heartbrokenly into it.

The D.A. looked at the girl as she lay there on the bed, weeping desperately. Finally he sat down beside her and gently lifted her dress up from her thighs. He saw a few pink streaks on her legs, and raised the dress higher over her buttocks. The portion of her behind that he could see was as pink as the panties which covered the part he could not see. Gently he pulled her drawers down and off under her knees as she twisted uneasily. He laid his hand on her behind, and Clara winced at the touch.

"Who whipped you?" he demanded.

"Men!" she sobbed. "Men . . . and then a girl." She abandoned the pillow for the comfort of his shoulder, resting gingerly on one buttock. He petted her reassuringly. "Three men," she whispered brokenly, "three men . . . with switches."

Conrad turned his eyes again to her blushing behind and hesitated. "It's probably no consolation to you," he said, "if I tell you that the whipping has made you look extremely desirable. That doesn't take the sting out of it, and I think that we ought to put something on it."

"There's . . . there's sunburn oil on the dressing table," Clara volunteered. "In the square bottle over there."

He secured it and sat down beside her again. "Just let me take your panties right off and lift your dress way up," he said, "then you can spread your legs out and relax. Just lie still." She had raised herself slightly to help him slip them off. "Now I'll put the oil on and rub it in."

"I should do it myself . . ." Clara objected weakly, as he began stroking her buttocks gently. "I don't want you to see all that."

"You couldn't do it as well," he soothed her. "I won't do it too hard . . . I'll be very careful." He worked his fingers smoothly over the oiled flesh, rubbing the grease into the horizontal lines that creased her thighs where her buttocks began. And perhaps a little unnecessarily he passed his hand between her thighs and rubbed there too.

"You might tell me how it happened," he questioned.

Clara wiped her tears away. The pain was beginning to ease and her bottom simply felt hot and glowing. But she was terribly conscious of the softness of her bottom and how freely it yielded as Conrad massaged it. He was making the cheeks jiggle, the way she could feel them jiggle when she ran, when her girlish breasts would jiggle too. She was not certain that she would not prefer the pain rather than the embarrassment of having him rub oil into her bare behind.

"I simply went to the door and knocked on it," she said. "It seemed as if that must be the right thing to do. And it was . . . too right."

The D.A. did not interrupt her. He was massaging her more briskly now, and instead of sitting beside her he was kneeling between her legs. This meant that they were spread wide apart, and Clara tried to keep her buttocks close together so that he could not see what lay between them. But the gentle massage made her muscles relax in spite of her endeavors.

"When I knocked, the door was opened at once, and a man took me by the arm and drew me inside." Clara went on. "There was only a dim light and for a couple of seconds I couldn't see much. Then I realized that there were three men in there, and that a naked woman was lying stretched out on the bed. She was lying very limply with one arm hanging over the edge of the bed, so I thought perhaps she had been drugged. But then she raised her head, and I saw that her ankles were in straps and fastened to the bottom of the bed. Her hands were free.

"Then there was another knock at the door, and the man let go of my arm to go and open it. A young girl came in. She was wearing a silk slack suit . . . I'm sure I've seen her around here before with Alice Burton. She saw me and came over and said, 'May I watch you . . . first . . . before my turn comes?'

"I was so confused by everything that I didn't know what to say, but I was afraid they might get suspicious if I was to hesitate, so I said 'Yes.' And the girl said, 'I'd like to help if it won't spoil it for you. It makes it better for me.'

"I just heard the words 'I'd like to help' so I said to her 'Thank you very much' without understanding anything about it at all.

"And then the girl said to me 'I always try to imagine how people will act. You probably like to pretend you hate it, don't you? Women as feminine as you usually do.' I hadn't the least idea what she was talking about, but I said 'Yes' again.

"Suddenly the man beside me said, 'Well, get on the bed, you little bitch, and we'll give it to you.' I didn't understand him a bit, and I just stood there not knowing what to do. Then another man said, 'Take off your clothes and get ready!' I stared at him and said, 'Take my clothes off? Oh! No!'

"The man beside me just laughed and grabbed me around the waist. 'If that's the way you like it, we'll take them off for you,' he said, and he picked me up and threw me onto the bed. Then I began to fight. But . . . but the other two came and helped him hold me down."

The D.A. gently rubbed Clara's behind. Some of the oil ran slowly down the deep crease between her buttocks, and his fingers followed it. "And you took off your clothes?" he asked. "All of them?"

"No, they did. Everything but my stockings. They took off my dress, and my brassiere, and then they pulled my panties down around my legs. And they fastened the straps around my ankles and rolled my stockings down to them too.

"I heard the girl say something, and I looked over at her. I thought she might help me. But she had taken off her slacks and was wearing only a brassiere and tennis shoes, so that her cunt was showing and everything. I begged the men to stop and let me go, but they just laughed at me. And one of them said to her, 'You can begin it if you want,' but she said to him, 'No, I'd sooner watch at first.'

115

"Then, while two of the men held my arms, the other got a switch and began to use it on my naked bottom. Oh! It was terrible. Not so much because it hurt. It only stung enough to make me jump, but the whole thing gave me such a dreadful sensation. Being there in the room with three men, and being naked and tied to the bed face down, and . . . thinking that maybe they would take their clothes off and rape me.

"I kept struggling and pleading with them all the time the first man was switching me. My buttocks began to smart like fire, and I felt that I was getting hot all over. The minutes seemed like hours before he stopped. And I thought it was all over then, but it wasn't. That was only the beginning."

Clara had lost the sense of her surroundings as she told her story, and the D.A. had unobtrusively become more and more free in his handling of her naked body. He had spread her legs further apart, and then a bit more again, and Clara had by degrees forgotten to keep her buttocks tense.

As a result she was quite as open and unprotected from both prying eyes and prying fingers as if she had deliberately laid herself open for display. Her pink cunt lay like a small sweet fruit between her creased thighs, and the D.A.'s fingers passed to and fro across it without once evoking the slightest protest. Between her bottom's reddened cheeks there was yet another rose-brown aperture towards which his fingers strayed. He rubbed gently between her cheeks, and along the deep crease, and Clara was conscious only of how soothing and yet exciting his oily fingertips had become.

"Then, as the man stopped, the girl came over to

the side of the bed," Clara went on. "When I looked up I saw that she had a switch in her hand too, and that she was smiling. She used the switch on the back of my thighs and between them. My legs were held apart by the straps on my ankles, and she could whip me wherever she wanted. I couldn't fight any longer. So I stopped trying to, and then they let go of my arms. I just lay there and squirmed on my stomach, and I wasn't able to turn and stop her switching my cunt because of the straps. She seemed to be switching me especially on my slit, and I was afraid I was bleeding . . . because I felt all wet there. I pleaded with her and promised her all sorts of crazy things, but she paid no attention to me.

"Suddenly she stopped and gave her switch to one of the men, and lay down across the bed at the foot of it. 'Do it to me now while I watch her,' she told him, and she kicked her shoes off and began to wiggle her bare toes as if in pleasant anticipation of it. The man began to beat her as hard as he could, not a bit like he had whipped me. And she commenced to moan and twist on the bed, and then she wriggled up alongside me and pressed her thigh between mine. Her sex was all wet, and it ran down my thigh too, and the whip was cutting right across us both.

"And then suddenly she jerked and gasped and quivered . . . and came all over me, and after a minute sat up and said to the men, 'Well, I guess our little friend has had enough to put her in condition for tonight by now.' So they untied my ankles, and I snatched up my undies and dress and began to struggle into them.

117

"The girl lay down again and stretched out across the bed and said, 'Now give me some more,' and she added to me, 'You can stay and watch if you like, and I'll suck you off while they do it.'

"She was terribly matter-of-fact saying a thing like that to me, but I said, 'No . . . I have to . . . to meet somebody.' That made them all laugh, but they opened the door and the man who had let me in slapped my behind as I went out. That made me jump . . . right out into the hall . . . and I came back here to you."

Clara suddenly realized that Conrad was not soothing her welts any longer. The place where his fingers nestled and were caressing was tender, but it was a tenderness created by nature and not by whip or switch, and if it were to be described as a welt it was one which fingering would never abate. He was just rubbing her ass-hole, rubbing it with short forward-poking strokes which made her feel frightfully queer in that part of her body.

"Stop it!" she cried. "What are you trying to do?"

Conrad poured a drop of the oil on her anus and said calmly, "You said she switched you here, didn't you?"

"Not there!" blushed Clara. "Between my legs, yes, but not there!"

"Then it must have been here." He began to rub her slit very gently. "It doesn't hurt now . . . not the least bit," she stammered as she tried to sit up on the bed.

"Oh! But it will if it isn't taken care of. Lie still and let me rub some more of this oil in it," Conrad insisted.

"I don't want you to. I don't care if it does hurt a

little bit. She didn't whip me there very hard." Clara tried once more to sit up. "Please stop!" she exclaimed. "I really don't want you to rub me there."

The D.A. pushed her firmly down on the bed once more. "But I'm going to rub it," he told her. "And what's more, I'm going to use what ought to be used for the job . . . and that is not fingers!" He leaned forward and unbuttoned his trousers, and Clara felt something softer and smoother and hotter and bigger than his fingers slide up between her thighs. "Now just don't struggle," he said, "for if you do something else might happen to you."

Clara pulled the pillow toward her and hid her face in it as she limply relaxed. At least it had no indignity to show her.

The D.A. tickled the most sensitive places between her legs with the tip of his prick. Then he tickled her cunt with it, more and more insistently. "Can you feel what I'm doing to you, Clara?" he demanded. Her silence made it necessary for him to persist, but finally he obtained the satisfaction of a stifled "Yes."

"That's good!" he said, "because now I'm going to tickle up your bottom, and I'm pretty sure you've never had that done before." And he thrust the oil-smeared tip of his throbbing weapon between the submissive girl's cheeks and ran it back and forth over the tight little entrance.

She couldn't even blush any more, she felt, for no blush would do the situation justice. She could feel his penis, hot and hard and oily, questing at her bottom with its plum-shaped tip, debauching a part of her whose very existence she hardly acknowledged, even when she used it in the normal way twice a day, in the privacy of her bathroom.

The D.A. continued his researches for several minutes, and gradually Clara realized that it was not altogether so unpleasant. Then he rubbed her slit in the same way, probing a little but never really attempting to enter. This delayed debauching of an innocent mind and body was a new thrill, and he wanted to extract every atom of interest and pleasure out of it before he achieved its culmination.

Finally, lying full length above the girl, he could rub at one stroke both the lips of her cunt with the tip of his prick and her anus with the shaft of it. He smiled down at her as he fancied . . . no, really felt . . . some movement of her lovely body in grudging response.

"Poor darling!" he said in pretended commiseration, "does it hurt much when I do this?"

"No!" Clara admitted doubtfully, "it doesn't hurt, but . . ."

"Hold your legs together more tightly," he whispered after a while. Clara did so, and began to enjoy the tight blows of his prick through the lips of her cunt and up against her little clitoris more and more, until suddenly and without warning . . . she came. There was no mistaking the flooding thrill and she could not deny it even to herself, and then before she knew what was happening and just as her spasm was dying down she felt a quick pain, and realized that his throbbing staff had thrust into her quivering body from behind.

"Ohh! No! Don't!" she screamed. "Take it out! Please, oh please take it out!" But Conrad took no notice of her entreaty and just kept it in place, moving his hips to and fro so that her buttocks quivered, and she felt that the depth of his cock in her bottom was titillating her nerves to ecstasy.

The pain did not go away, but in a moment or two Clara came again. She felt as if she were going crazy, and then she suddenly realized that he had come too, and while his sperm welled up inside her his fingers clutched at her breasts and her throbbing clitoris, and he began to fuck wildly in and out of her behind.

She screamed again and again, but on a high note that rose from pain to pleasure as her sensations overcame her. She could no longer tell whether the pain or the pleasure was the greater. Her sensations rose and rose and spread and spread, from her breasts and her cunt and her bottom, and suddenly all her muscles were agonizingly taut and she spent again.

A long while later, it seemed, she hardly felt anything in her bottom, but he was still there, only quite soft now. She tried tightening her muscles. It worked like a charm. His prick popped out with a sucking sound, and the backwash of his spend trickled down over her dripping cunt.

Chapter 10

"*Shall* we begin with wine or something stronger?" asked Conrad as they went downstairs. "The people you meet are in many ways determined at parties by what you drink, as I found out long ago."

"Let's start with the wine, then, that ought to lead us to mild people," Clara riposted.

"I don't know about that," said the D.A. as they poured themselves two glasses of claret and looked around. "Now take that girl in shorts and such charming legs. Too bad she's drinking something pink and with ice in it. Ah! Here's something better!" A girl with a red velvet gown cut so low that it displayed her breasts nearly to the nipples was approaching. She was sipping a red wine too.

"But here," Clara replied, "is something better yet. The lady with the scorpion tattooed on her stomach."

Alice Burton smiled as they approached her. "Well, my dear," she said, "I have been looking for you all evening." Clara introduced Conrad as Mr. Douglas, and felt a quick spurt of jealousy as she saw how Mrs. Burton immediately annexed him, and seemed to be already considering him as a possible bed companion. She wondered if she could be really jealous. And then she wished she were more mature-looking and sexy.

"We were just speculating on the possibility of some

sort of entertainment," the D.A. said as he shook hands.

"I believe they're throwing some male poets to the Lesbians right now," said Mrs. Burton. "But are you serious?" she added.

"Completely," replied Conrad. "Let us eat, drink, and be merry, for who knows what tomorrow may bring!" He bowed to her.

"Then we go this way," Alice answered, taking one of his arms and leaving Clara to take the other. She was feeling a bit light-headed from the wine, and swayed a little as Conrad said, "But we must have something more to drink, give me your glasses and I'll fetch it for you."

"Your friend is charming," observed Mrs. Burton as he vanished down the passage. She sat down on the couch and passed her arm around Clara's waist. "I suppose I don't need to ask if he is your most intimate friend?" She glanced about the room and suddenly knelt down before Clara. "Quick, raise your dress for me," she whispered softly. "Quickly, quickly."

"But not here!" said Clara urgently. "You can't do it here! It's impossible!"

"I must!" Alice insisted. She raised the skirt above Clara's thighs. "Let me kiss you there for just a moment. It will taste so delightful with the wine."

"But he'll come back!" Clara warned.

"He will if you keep arguing about it!" She thrust the dress all the way up and pressed her face against Clara's bare belly. Clara wondered why she had forgotten to put on her panties. She remembered that she had no brassiere on either. Only a garter belt for her underwear. "You must let me lick you once before he has you," Alice continued. "Last night I slept with you and had you, and tonight he will."

"He will not!" Clara exclaimed impetuously.

Alice pushed the younger girl's legs apart and kissed the hair over her sex. The tip of her tongue curled around and down and into her cunt. The slit opened softly, and poor Clara shuddered, but not with cold or even with distaste. It was so terribly exciting, and she could not deny it.

"Rub your slit against my tongue," pleaded Alice, and Clara spread her knees and sank her hips a little, pressing her cunt back and forth over the woman's mouth. Both her sex and the seeking mouth were as wet and slippery as a peeled plum. "Please let me stop," she begged finally, "I'm sure I can hear him coming."

To Clara it seemed only a few seconds later that he appeared, and she felt that everything which had happened must be written all too clearly on her face. She blushed to her ears at the thoughts which flashed through her mind. But Conrad gave no sign that he had noticed anything unusual.

"This way," said Alice Burton coolly, leading them to a small door in the corner, and through it to a tiny private theater, whose seating accommodation consisted of couches and pillows, with screens angled onto a balcony railing. Down on the lower level was a pit illuminated by soft lights, and as they sank onto the cushions three figures entered the arena.

A lone girl ran to the center of the pit and threw herself prone on the cushions there. Red hair fell like flame around her shoulders, and except for a pale yellow scarf that hung down her body and between her thighs she was completely naked. Two men followed her, one in beach pajamas and the other in a bathing singlet. They were tanned brown and appeared to be in their early twenties.

As the girl rolled sensuously on the cushions one of the men snatched the scarf from her body, and she lay before them completely naked, her legs sprawled apart, and her red-haired crotch bare and tempting. She did not have a V of hair to hide her slit, but rather a thin down that reached from her cunt half way up to her navel.

Clara closed her eyes as the men sank down onto the soft rugs alongside the girl in the pit. "The situation is becoming quite interesting," murmured the D.A. as he leaned over Clara and made her look up. "Don't look away now, I want you to watch this!"

The two men were sharing the girl with their caresses. They stroked her thighs and her naked belly, tickling her with their fingers. Her clenched fists thrust deeply into the soft pillows beneath her, and she raised her slim body, rubbing her thighs against the men. Her nipples were hard and erect. She turned and rubbed them against the body of the blond man, at the same time pressing her buttocks into the crotch of the other. Then she leaned over the first one, letting her breasts brush across his chest, and as she did so she slipped her hand beneath the waistband of his trousers.

She let herself be turned over on her stomach by him, and lay between his legs, feeling in his trousers and raising her buttocks while the curly-haired blond fingered her crotch. The dark man was tickling the soles of her little pink feet. She slid one hand up the trouser leg of the blond, who twisted with excitement at her daring caress.

"Please let's go now!" Clara whispered, feeling sure that everyone was looking at the blushes that covered her face and ran down her neck as far as her bosom. She felt that she would scream with excitement in a minute

"No! Drink your wine," Conrad said. He pulled her hand into his lap and pressed it against his prick. He held it there, curling her fingers around it, and making her pass her hand back and forth along its stiff length.

The girl in the pit had opened the trousers of the blond man by now. She pulled them down while he lifted his hips to help her. She ran her fingers through the curly hair around his cock, and then lowered her head and took his soft sex wholly into her mouth. The dark man in the trunks took them off, and when the girl saw him naked she abandoned her first victim and turned and began to lick his prick instead. Suddenly she threw herself on her back and lay there with one hand in the crotch of each man, rubbing their pricks and squeezing their testicles.

The blond was the first to mount her. He rolled her over and threw himself between her thighs, pressing his sex into her crotch. He thrust violently upward and entered her. He drew back and thrust once more, while the girl exclaimed passionately, "Harder, harder."

The thrust that followed really took her breath away, and for a moment she was silent as he commenced to fuck her in real earnest. But then she again gasped "Harder!" and locked her legs about the thighs of her lover, while at the same time she turned her head around questioningly until she found the dark man beside her and began to caress his prick and balls with eager lips.

Clara, her hands trembling, thirstily swallowed the last of her wine. Conrad surprised her then by taking her hand from his lap. But as he did so he slipped his own hand under her taut skirt and up her thigh. No panties. He ran his finger around her cunt and then began feeling it and slipping his fingers between the moist folds. Clara slid her bottom forward on her cushion so as to open herself more fully to his caress.

"Here, give me your hand," the D.A. whispered to Clara. Her fingers jerked back nervously as they touched naked flesh once more, but Conrad had his way. His prick was not out of his pants entirely and he made her take it in her fingers and rub it gently up and down. His own fingers went back to her cunt, and slipped in until they could tickle her clitoris.

The men in the pit were still taking turns with the red-headed girl, and a spreading puddle of spend had appeared between her thighs, until she moved a pillow to cover it. Clara thought it was impossible that any girl . . . even a red-head . . . could be so passionate and abandoned with other people watching. Well, not quite incredible, she decided, for there she was. Clara was hot all over, she felt nervous and excited, and she no longer made any pretense of not watching the performance.

The men were relaxed on the cushions now . . .

fucked out, and the girl was stretched out on her stomach before them, one leg thrown across each of them. She took one man's prick in her hand and the other in her mouth, and wriggled her bare toes as though she were in ecstasy.

Conrad gently removed Clara's hand from his sex. She had not realized till then how unreservedly she had been . . . and still was pulling on it, as she watched the spectacle in the pit.

She twisted her hands together in her lap, ashamed and embarrassed, and tried to shrink away from Conrad's fingers in her slit. She decided to squeeze her legs together and stop him from playing with her sex, but for some unexplained reason she put off the decision from minute to minute as she watched the scene in the pit.

One of the men down below stood up, and the naked girl turned to him on her knees. He thrust his cock to her mouth, and she flung her arms around him. With passionate moans she began sucking his prick so deliberately that it was evident she wanted him to come in her mouth. Clara leaned forward in tense anticipation. Suddenly the girl jerked the man's knees to her breasts with all her strength. He thrust his prick at her with a savagery that almost knocked her down. Clara almost cried out, but clenched her hands against her lips in time to smother it.

"More wine?" the D.A. asked Clara calmly, and handed his own glass to her. She squeezed it until it almost shattered, in her endeavor to control the shaking of her hands. Conrad stopped feeling her sex long enough to raise her dress up over her tense hips.

She felt that he was publicly undressing her, though no one a foot away would have seen anything in that dim light.

And she felt too, that like the girl in the pit, she was on her knees. She glanced back at the girl, who was now holding one of her soft breasts in each hand and smearing their nipples' pink loveliness in a lustful caress. Reaching upward with her torso, she was rubbing them gently on the tip of the prick she had been sucking.

Clara felt her own nipples harden, and she lifted a hand and touched them through her dress. Maybe she should have worn a brassiere, she thought. She watched the sway of the girl's hips down there in the pit, and her own buttocks unconsciously swung in sympathy. She put one hand over Conrad's caressing fingers at her sex, leaving the other gently squeezing her taut young breasts. Her excitement was becoming uncontrollable as the scene below mounted to its climax.

The red-headed girl thrust her mouth again toward the man's crotch. He drew slowly away from her. She held his cock in one hand and caressed it with the other, creeping after him on her knees across the thick rug. She drew her shoulders down and pleaded with her whole body, reaching again for his prick with her eager mouth. The whole audience heard her whisper in agonized tones, "Please . . . please . . . ."

Clara could have wept for the girl's humility. Her own lips silently formed the word as the girl bent forward once more . . . "Please . . ."

This time the man let her have it. She thrust the

swollen sex into her mouth and sucked it eagerly, fiercely, tossing her head from side to side as she did so. Her hair fell down over her face, and she paused for a moment to fling it back with one hand. Clara ran her hand through her own hair, and pressed her crotch forward against Conrad's fingers. She felt smothered and faint and giddy.

Something was happening to her . . . her thighs were taut and her stomach shuddered, while her breath came gaspingly and her breasts swelled and hardened. Suddenly she realized that she was coming. Conrad seemed to know it too, for the finger in her cunt moved faster and faster and pinched and caressed the tip of her clitoris and the folds of her slit. Clara gasped audibly as she watched the sudden plunging rape of the girl's mouth and the sucking avid taking of the man's sperm. She closed her eyes and pressed her own cunt against Conrad's fingers. Her hearing numbed, her tongue clove to the roof of her mouth . . . and she quivered frantically as her love juice poured down.

Clara crumpled against the D.A.'s chest, her face the mask of one who was in a daze. She brushed the back of her slim hand across her eyes, and he steadied her in his arms, for she seemed ready to faint.

"Rita," she said weakly, "I've got to find her . . ."

"I think we'd better leave," Conrad said, "and anyhow we can't talk here. We'll discuss it in your bedroom."

Upstairs in her room he closed the door behind him and stood looking down at her. "Well?" he queried.

Clara seated herself on the edge of the bed. "Well, what and where and how?" she inquired.

"Right now I think you should get some sleep," Conrad remarked equably.

"Well, I don't. I'm going to look for Rita right now."

"Do I have to put you to bed by force?" Conrad asked her in resigned tones.

Clara set her teeth and stamped a ridiculously small foot in an attempt to be firm. "I think it's time you realized that I do not like this overbearing attitude that you so often adopt!" she said indignantly.

"Disgusting, isn't it?" he agreed. "Nevertheless, you are going to bed." He picked her up in his arms and laid her on the bed. Clara immediately tried to escape by rolling off on the other side. He dragged her back and pulled her dress up over her head, imprisoning her arms. Then he slipped off her shoes and removed her stockings. Bare-legged, Clara writhed and gasped out unintelligible insults.

"If you aren't quiet," Conrad warned her, "I am going to give your little pink behind a spanking." He turned her over and gently smacked her bare buttocks with his hand, pulling down her garter belt. "You don't want to make me do that, do you?" And then he was silent so long while his hand lay there caressingly on her bottom that Clara, from beneath the folds of her dress, became uneasy.

"What are you doing now?" she asked doubtfully as she wiggled her body into a more comfortable position.

"Looking at you," he said. "What else would I be doing?" He let his hand slide along her hip and slither down between her legs.

"Don't," said Clara. "Let me sit up. I don't like you to look at me that way when I can't see you. Let me up!"

"By no means. I like you this way," the D.A. countered. He took a tuft of Clara's sex-hair in his fingers and gently tugged at it. "Very soft and pretty," he remarked.

"I can't breathe," objected Clara. "I'm smothering down here like this."

"I'll let you up," he said, "but not just yet." He ran his arm between her legs and up under her belly, hugging her buttocks against him. "If you were any riper you'd burst and spill all over my fingers, wouldn't you?" And then he added, "Can you guess what I'm looking at now?"

Clara jerked her legs together and squeezed the fleshy part of her thighs against each other. "You're clairvoyant," Conrad told her, "but I can still see in. In fact . . ."

"What did you do?" Clara exclaimed suddenly. She rolled over and sat up, and the D.A. pulled her dress up over her softly rounded shoulders. "What did you do?" she repeated.

"I kissed it," he said coolly. "Here, lie back and let me do it again from the front. It's much easier that way."

"I'm going to bed now," Clara said hurriedly her face crimson as she tried to slip away from him.

"You change your mind so quickly," he said, holding her to him by slipping an arm about her waist and hips, "that I am beginning to believe that you have no real convictions. I don't believe that you want to go to sleep yet, Clara. I think you want to lie here on the bed and let me play with your pussy for a little while, and kiss it . . . and kiss you . . . all over."

He arranged a pillow for her head in such a manner that her shoulders were raised and she could look down at him as he bent toward her cunt.

"Why can't you leave me alone?" she whispered in a faint voice. "Just for a little while . . . until I get some rest and . . ." His lips brushed the hair of her muff, and she quickly clasped her hands over it. "Please don't do it again yet," she begged.

The D.A. leaned on one arm and persuasively pulled one of her round knees away from its mate. "Didn't you like it the first time?" he asked. "I mean when Alice Burton did it?" he went on before she could answer. He reached up between her thighs and plucked at the hair which half concealed the lips of her cunt, and the rosy petals parted with a tiny audible sound like a kiss. After a minute he went on, "I won't insist on an answer to that question, but I do insist on having the same privileges that you allowed Alice."

"Please . . . please don't . . ." Clara murmured. She put her hand on his head to push him away, but the strength seemed to ebb from her arm as she felt his warm breath stir her pussy. Her fingers tightened in his hair and his lips slipped up over her thigh. "No . . . no further," she whispered.

With his face pressed against her thigh he looked up at her face over the tips of her heaving breasts. While

133

Clara watched him he took a bit of the flesh of her thigh in his teeth and nipped it. He made her spread her legs farther apart and gazed into her crotch with sparkling eyes.

"Don't look at me that way," she protested softly, "it makes me feel like an animal."

"What a lovely animal you make," he murmured, "and what a tempting little split treasure you carry between your legs and bottom."

Clara slipped one hand between her legs to cover her slit, but he pushed it gently away. "Don't come any nearer," she pleaded.

"Only near enough to kiss it," he said. He crept upward toward her cunt with his lips, dragging them caressingly over her heated thighs. Clara twisted her naked body as though she lay on thorns.

"No nearer," she begged. "Ohhh . . . No!" The wine in her veins whispered deceitfully to her senses. She tangled her fingers in Conrad's hair and tried to push him away with both hands. But her arms seemed made of rubber, and they fell back, pulling his mouth closer to her instead of thrusting it away. His lips touched the dark crown of hair around her cunt lips and she shivered. She was ashamed of her nakedness and her sex, ashamed that he was a man and wanted her body and was so close to having it. Shame crept along her thighs where his head pressed between them, and she felt desire drain from his fingers into her legs and up past her thighs into her moist and defenseless opening.

Hunger for the touch of his mouth throbbed through her every sense and she was ashamed for the irresistible force which swept down her defenses and stole her from herself.

Conrad was kissing her slit, pressing the lips open by turning his head from side to side. The hair spread and the lips of her sex swelled against the lips of his warm mouth. Her cunt felt hot and flushed. It was changing color from pink to dusky red. He kissed it with a smacking sound, and then he kissed it again, low down in the wet open part between her buttocks.

Clara's legs writhed, but she could not make them move her away from him. He slid his arms under her hips and lifted them to kiss her solidly in the cunt. Clara saw his eyes shut, watched his mouth press into the thick tangle of curls and crush against her, while it seemed as though fire raced through her veins, burning at her heart. His tongue slipped once more across her sex. She shut her eyes and her head rolled from side to side on the pillow. She began to press herself to him . . . spreading her thighs and pulling up her knees, opening her cunt to his tongue.

"How can you . . . do that? Oh . . . do that!" she moaned. She rubbed her crotch against his chin and he licked her, curling his tongue around her clitoris and prodding open the butterfly wings of her tender cunt lips with his tongue-tip. Then it stabbed into her like a dagger, wringing a cry of ecstasy from her lips.

The pointed tip of his tongue thrust stiffly into the opening of her cunt, and Clara twisted on her hips to press it in further. She was swept up in a tidal wave of excitement, and she reached out her hands blindly to touch his hard male body. She seized his trousers and pulled them open anyhow. Her hands slipped in at both sides of his crotch, luxuriating in the moist sweaty warmth of the hair and the groove of his sex, and she clutched firmly at his swelling prick. He twisted his hips and gave his cock more freedom as she pulled at it, and then her searching fingers drew out his balls too.

She hugged her body to his, pressing her breasts against the throbbing organ she was holding as he twisted his hips around toward her shoulders. Suddenly Clara realized that she was rubbing her nipples on the head of his prick just as the girl in the pit had done earlier in the evening. "No more," she whispered, trying to push him away and sit up.

Conrad took his cock in one hand and smeared it across her face. "Kiss it," he said, plucking his lips from her cunt. "Lick it if you want me to go on kissing you." Clara quivered as the swollen gland slid across her lips. "Kiss it," insisted his voice again. Then his tongue curled warmly into her cunt once more, warmly enough to melt even a firmer resolution than hers. She kissed the tip of his prick and began to caress it with the flat of her tongue. She licked its nakedness and its hairiness too, taking it into her own hands and pushing his hands away. She licked it from top to bottom, and let her tongue absorb the wetness that collected at the top, meanwhile jutting her hips back and forth and around as his hands were guiding them to do.

Then Conrad took his prick in his own hand again. Clara's hot tongue licked his fingers as it sought his cock, but she did not stop. She pushed her tongue between his fingers, and over and around them, until she realized that he was pushing the swollen weapon

136

insistently against her half open lips. Then she turned her head away, frightened of what he had been wordlessly demanding of her. And then he asked her again, this time not wordlessly.

Clara shook her head, not looking at him, and she said appealingly, "Let's go on . . . doing what we were doing . . ." She trailed off into silence. Her boldness, the lascivious heated sound of her own voice frightened her. For a moment she felt herself to be two people, one a horror-stricken observer . . . that was her real self, and the other a young girl who was quivering and squirming and whispering as she lay across the bed in this lewd, clutching embrace with a man.

"You must do it to me," he insisted. He caressed her warm buttocks and squeezed them tightly. "Before you do it to someone else," he added. The implicit assurance made Clara's heart pound with shame. But she returned to the subject as a moth returns to the flame, to finally scorch its wings. "I will never do it to someone else," she said indignantly. "Or to you either!" she added. His mocking smile seared her sharply, and she stared miserably at him.

"I think you will," he said. He touched her mouth with the tip of his cock and said, "Lick it. Go on. You'll hardly know when it slips in if you're licking it already."

Clara didn't want to do it. But somehow her tongue did slip out and caress the swollen organ once more. She rubbed the tip of her tongue over it, and although it pressed into her lips she did not stop. She kept caressing it with her tongue until it had pressed in so deeply between her lips that she could no longer

137

pretend that she didn't have the red head in her mouth. Conrad pressed down slightly and the whole tip of his cock slid slowly in and she closed her lips around it.

A voice seemed to whisper softly in Clara's ear. It was the echo of the voice of the girl she had watched with the two men in the pit. "Please," it said, "Please . . ." This thing she was now doing was what the girl had begged for so abjectly. Clara closed her eyes and sucked as the voice changed and now became her own. She twined her arms around Conrad's buttocks and hugged him closely to her. His prick was almost choking her, but she kept on sucking fiercely. He thrust his tongue back into her slit and began to suck her too, shaking his head wildly from side to side between her thighs.

His hips began to jerk to and fro and he dragged his cock in and out of her mouth, while she kept trying to lick her tongue around the tip and retain it when it thrust inward. His movements became faster yet, and her senses swam. Her sex was burning and heat seemed to be licking all around her. Her jaws ached and her tongue was sore. She tensed her body and rubbed her cunt wildly against his tongue, and then spent ecstatically just as her own mouth was flooded with his sperm. It jetted and jetted up against her throat in hot bursts. His hips were still holding her head in position, and there seemed to be nothing she could do but swallow . . . or choke.

After an hour or more Clara was still awake, remembering what had passed between them. The salty, biting taste she must admit was not so bad after all.

She kept thinking how strange it had been when the hot flow had welled into her mouth as if he were bleeding into her. Her body was tired but unsatisfied. The longer she lay there the more wide awake she became. And finally she got up and began to dress.

Chapter 11

Clara went downstairs. As she hesitated in the hall a girl came abruptly through the door and bumped into her. "I'm sorry," she exclaimed, clutching Clara's arm, "I wasn't really looking where I was going."

"It was my fault for standing in the passageway," said Clara, smiling back at the girl, whom she remembered having seen in the garden that morning.

And as naturally as though they had been lifelong friends the girl took Clara by the arm and said, "Let's go together, shall we?"

"Why, yes," said Clara, a bit bewildered. They walked on down the corridor toward the little private theater, and then fumbled their way to one of the loges in the semi-darkness.

"You've never been in the pit, have you?" the girl asked casually as they seated themselves on a couch. Clara was so staggered by the question that she could hardly control her voice sufficiently to answer in the negative. "Have you?" she queried in return.

"Just once," the girl admitted. "I wanted to see what it felt like to perform in front of an audience."

Clara remembered how she had felt when Johnny had taken her in the arbor before only two people. And this girl calmly admitted to having had an audience. She shivered a little. "What was it like?" she asked. "I mean . . . down there?"

"Fun enough so that I'll probably try it again," the girl said casually. "There was another girl too, and four men. We took on two at the time, and then three, and finally four. But the position you get into with four of them is too silly." She smiled reminiscently.

"But didn't you feel awfully ashamed?" Clara queried, still puzzled by the girl's sang-froid.

"Of course I did," the girl admitted. "I expected to. And perhaps that was what thrilled me as much as anything."

"That's just what frightened me," Clara confided, as she raised her voice above the music. "All this is terribly exciting but I don't want to be excited by it. I think it is terrible that I should like doing these things."

The girl was leaning very close to her. She ran her tanned fingers up Clara's arm and across her breasts in an enticing caress as she answered her. "I don't think a person can choose what things will be exciting to them." Clara felt that there was a great deal of truth in this, and she also thought that she had heard it before somewhere. The girl still stroked Clara's arm, and her warm thigh pressed insinuatingly against her leg. After several seconds the girl spoke again in a quiet coaxing voice. "Don't you know how to ask me? Is that what the trouble is?"

"I don't understand," said Clara, puzzled but strangely moved by the alluring tones in which the girl had spoken.

The girl took Clara's hand and placed it on her thigh, and she was surprised to find that all her leg was bare. "You know I like you," the girl was whispering, "I'll say yes . . ."

"Yes, what?" Clara asked, but the girl did not answer that query.

"You can slip your hand all the way up," she said. "I'm not wearing anything underneath, not even a bra. It's such a nuisance taking things off and putting them on again, don't you think?" She gently drew Clara's hand along her thigh toward her hip, and Clara's fingers involuntarily tightened as they slid over the smooth contours of her rounded buttocks.

"You needn't be so timid about feeling me," the girl said. "I knew right along that it would end up this way. If I hadn't liked you I shouldn't have stayed. You haven't done it very often yet, have you?" she concluded.

Clara was as still as a nestling bird. She was just beginning to understand what the other girl meant, but she did not quite know what she should do next. She let her hand be drawn up into the other girl's crotch, and she shivered as if with a sudden fever.

"How often have you done it?" the girl persisted.

"Done what?" Clara whispered, knowing quite well what the answer would be.

"Loved another girl. Done what you're thinking about doing to me." The girl slipped an arm around Clara's shoulder and held her close while she herself slid backward and down on the couch. Clara found herself lying over the girl, breast to breast, with one hand under the girl's skirt and the other by her head, half covered by her thick blonde hair.

"I wasn't thinking of doing anything," Clara whispered. She could only see the girl's deep brown eyes looking clearly and passionately into her own. The girl rubbed her breasts across Clara's and hugged her closer.

"You're so timid that I'd almost believe you if I hadn't seen you with Alice Burton this morning. Did she break you in? Or was there someone before her?" She slipped her hands under Clara's dress and between her lower thighs. She parted her own legs a bit more and pulled up her skirt still further, and said, "I stayed with Alice for a week once. She was awfully nice."

"With Mrs. Burton?" Clara exclaimed. "Then she ...you ..."

"Lie closer," the girl said. "Do you want me to tell you about it?"

"No! Don't tell me. She doesn't mean anything to me," Clara interjected.

"I didn't realize you felt that way about her," the girl said sympathetically. "Loving people is . . ."

"I don't love her," cried Clara almost hysterically ... "I just don't want to hear what you did because . . . because I'm so terribly ashamed of what I did. . . ."

"Then she was the first one!" the girl cried triumphantly. "I knew it. But why are you so frightened and bashful now? No one is going to bite you for loving me. Put your hand between my legs. Do you want me to open my clothes so that you can have my breasts too?"

"Please don't talk that way . . . not so loud," Clara said pleadingly. "Someone is bound to hear us." She felt the girl's fingers slip up her thighs, and then she sighed something quite unintelligible in her ear. Clara let the girl pull her dress higher and higher, until it

143

could go no further unless the snap was unfastened. Her bare stomach felt the warm touch of the girl's hot belly, and her thighs were pressed against the girl at the juncture of her soft groin.

"You're ashamed, aren't you?" the girl whispered, as she drew Clara closer. "You're so ashamed that I can feel it. It's in the way that you touch me, in the sound of your breath, in the beat of your heart when I lay my hand on your breasts." The rhythm of her words fascinated Clara's imagination until they sank deeply and indelibly into her memory. "You're ashamed of wanting me," the girl concluded softly.

Clara took a handful of the girl's cunt-hair and let it slide springily through her fingers. "I never wanted to do anything like this before," she said. "I always thought that only girls who wore their hair short and sported neckties did this sort of thing."

"Fuck me!" the girl whispered in a tiny sibilant voice. "Go on, fuck me the way Alice taught you to fuck her!" She drew Clara closer between her lovely spread thighs and raised her hips. Clara rubbed her crotch against the girl's with a very gentle, modest motion of her hips, and then, swept by a confused shame, she buried her face against the girl's soft shoulder.

"Fuck me some more," the girl insisted. "I could hardly feel that."

Clara pressed her cunt against the other girl's cunt, rubbing her juice-wetted hair into the unfamiliar slit. The girl writhed closer against her. "Ohhh! How that stings and burns," the girl gasped, sucking in her breath. She pressed still closer, so that the little inner petals of Clara's cunt touched hers. "Now we're kissing with our downstairs mouth," she said. "Kiss me harder."

They rolled their sexes silently together for a moment, pressing their slits across each other to make the union more exciting. "In a little while I'll let you kiss me down there with your real mouth," the girl promised, and she opened her dress and Clara's and touched Clara's taut nipples with her own. Her fingers slipped up between Clara's buttocks and deftly dipped into her cunt. Clara gasped. "Is Alice Burton the only woman you ever did this with?" the girl inquired.

"Ohhh! Yes!" sighed Clara, almost too busy to answer. "I never thought I'd do it with any other woman," she went on after a moment. Then she continued, "Are you sure that no one can see us? If the lights go on . . ."

"No one can see us, and the lights won't go on," the girl reassured her. She held Clara's head in the crook of her arm and rubbed her nipples over Clara's cheeks and eyes and nose and lips.

"You haven't tasted my nipples yet," she said. And she made Clara touch them with the tip of her tongue, plucking at first one and then the other, till they hardened like two red cherries.

Clara pulled her mouth away after a moment. "You won't tell anyone about this, will you?" she pleaded. "Promise me that you won't tell Alice Burton!" She coaxed the girl with her whole body, scarcely realizing the wantonness of her own gesture. She fucked the girl as she herself would secretly have liked to be fucked, rubbing her cunt lips . . . one and then both of them . . . between the girl's, and squeezing her buttocks with one hand while the fingers of the other probed into her cunt.

"It'll be our own secret," the girl promised, and she thrust her fingers back into Clara's sex, squeezing her as she gave a little jump at the entrance of the long middle finger. "No one will ever know," she went on. "Here, let me rub my finger around and around inside you while you fuck me. Open your cunt the way you do when a man fucks you."

Clara drew nearer to the girl, curving her body to fit the other woman's sensual mold. "I never had that happen," she confessed. "I haven't ever really . . . been fucked . . . yet!"

The darkness was really silent for a minute. Then the girl's voice asked slowly, "Are you joking?" and paused for an answer. "No!" said Clara, "I'm not joking. I almost have been, but never really."

There was a long silence again, and then the girl said, "Do you know what? I'm blushing. And I haven't blushed in years. Whatever is wrong with the man you're going around with now. Let me talk to him and I'll remind him of what a man ought to do with a lovely girl like you." She petted Clara's plump bottom and added, "I didn't know girls could be so nice and bitchy when they were still virgins." Clara felt the girl close her thighs fiercely on her own hips as she thrust her whole hand deep into Clara's sex and caressed it feverishly.

"I shouldn't have told you," Clara whispered. "It makes me seem worse for doing this, doesn't it?" She glanced briefly into the other girl's eyes. "You can't realize how ashamed I am, and how something makes me do this just the same . . . Ohhh! Let me up before the lights come on!"

The girl released Clara for a moment and moved further into the corner of the couch, embracing Clara with her bare thighs and pulling her head lower. When her cheek touched her belly Clara let her nose slip down into the other's muff. "Kiss my cunt with your mouth the way you kissed it with your cunt," the girl prompted.

Clara's lips touched curly hair, softer and rather less plentiful than Alice Burton's, and the sweetly odorous scent of the girl's moist sex startled her. Her hand was lying on the girl's thigh and both hand and limb were trembling. She was panting, and her head drooped forward with a strange kind of weakness. Her arms slid up along the girl's hips and Clara fell forward, rubbing her breasts on the girl's naked thighs. Her lips found the long, pouting slit, and she kissed it.

She could see almost nothing. She could find the leaf-shaped shadow of hair on the girl's smooth belly, and she could see the spot on the girl's thighs where her stockings made them seem darker, but of what lay between the spread legs she could discern nothing at all. Shadows, deep, impenetrable, masked the blonde girl's deep crotch from any intimacy but that of lips.

"Fuck me with your mouth," the girl whispered softly. "You should be able to do it better with your mouth than with your cunt." She rubbed her crotch over Clara's cheeks and pulled her head down closer to complete the caress. Clara put her lips eagerly to the sugar-sweet sex, tasting the tiny wet lips inside it as she pursed her lips and pushed inward. Her mouth

147

trembled nervously as though protesting against this wanton embrace, but she forced herself to penetrate yet deeper. Then she became submissively still, keeping her mouth pressed there tightly while the lovely blonde fucked fiercely against its moist warmth.

The girl groped for Clara's breasts and tickled their erect nipples. "Now I want you to fuck me with these stiff little pricks," she said, gently pinching them. "You'll have to press yourself very close to me, but if you try hard you can get them into my cunt." The proposal seemed the depths of humiliation to Clara, and she strained away from the girl's embrace. Her breasts prickled as though their abuse had already been consummated.

The girl laughed quietly in the dark. "I can see that Alice didn't have you for very long," she said, "if you haven't learned to use your nipples on another girl's cunt." She paused and then added, "I'm sorry we didn't go to my room instead of here. I'd have loved to see those little prick-ends as they'll be, wet and stiff, when you've run them through my cunt, and then let me suck them clean. I like my own smell, don't you? Like your own smell, I mean? Not mine. I can see you like that all right."

Clara was wondering about that, when she discovered that beneath the other girl's feminine gentleness there was a quite forceful will as well.

Quite firmly she was made to bend forward and press her torso and breasts between the girl's thighs. Her nipples just touched the cunt-hair, which tickled them a little, and then they were thrust up against the warm spread slit. Clara felt her whole breast made

wet by the other girl's dripping cunt, and she shrank
back in sudden bashfulness. But the girl pushed her
shoulders around until the other breast had dipped its
nipple too.

"Push them way in," the girl ordered softly, and
Clara obeyed. Submissively she gave first one and then
the other of her hardening nipples to the open lips,
forcing them into the hole and rubbing them back
and forth and up and down as they slipped out under
the other girl's squirming. Clara's breasts had never
felt so sensitive, but she squeezed them in and about
until they ached, driven by some perverse passion
which the humiliation aroused in her.

"When you go to your room," the girl sighed unsteadily, "put a drop of perfume on your nipples. Just
a touch, that makes the scent sort of confusing. Now
you'd better lick me," she went on. "We haven't much
more time I'm afraid."

Weak and trembling from the emotional effects of
her debauchery, Clara meekly stroked the girl's cunt
with her wet tongue. She caressed the pouting lips
and passed her mouth over the dripping cunt and
between the spread thighs, breathing excitedly when
she could get her nose up out of the girl's muff far
enough to exhale. Affection that was more than affection flooded her. She felt that she wanted to do
anything that the girl might ask of her. Anything at all.

She used her lips and her tongue shamelessly, sucking in the tiny cunt-lips and the sex-hair and holding
them in her mouth while she shook her head from
side to side against the girl's lifting and falling crotch.
With one finger she tickled the girl's clitoris, keeping

her forefinger out of the way of her caressing tongue and lips.

"Follow my fingers with your tongue," the girl demanded, slipping her hands into her crotch and rubbing her cunt lips up and down against each other and across Clara's tongue for a brief moment, before she let her fingers wander. She led Clara's lips up into the thicket of her blonde curly pussy, and down along her soft inner thighs, and into her cunt again. Clara stroked her tongue along the delicious route, reaching forward with the tip to touch the girl's cunt-tasting fingers to discover where they were leading her. The girl drew one knee up and lifted her buttocks. "Hurry!" she whispered, as she proffered Clara the smooth curves, "Here! Here!"

Clara's lips brushed across the hot, smooth skin of the girl's buttocks. "Now kiss them!" the girl demanded. Clara glued her mouth to the girl's bottom, hugging the raised thigh while she kissed the rounded buttocks. Then she was told to pass her tongue around and across each of them. The wetness of her tongue dried to coolness on the flesh, and the girl began to wriggle with a passionate chill. She drew her fingers into the dark crease between her plump mounds, helping to guide Clara's head there with the other hand. Then, as she touched her anus, she covered it.

Clara licked up to the tips of the girl's fingers and stopped. "Ask me to take my fingers away," the girl whispered. "Let me hear you say . . . please?"

Clara rested her cheek between the girl's hot buttocks, her lips brushing the crinkly hair between them

She was so overwrought that her breath came as short, tight sobs. "I can't say that, and I can't do it either," she pleaded, blushing crimson. "Ohh! No, not that!"

"You can say it and you can do it," the girl replied, "and if you don't hurry the lights are going to come on again."

For a moment Clara thought she was willing to, but then she discovered that she just couldn't. She clung closer to the girl's naked, palpitating thighs. She had thought that she could do anything for this girl, that she could give her any sort of caress that she might desire, but now that she was faced with the reality the plunge seemed too great. She tried to imagine what it would be like to do as the girl asked, to replace the shielding fingers with her own lips, to kiss that little crinkled aperture in the girl's bottom with her tongue, and she discovered that her imagination was too vivid to permit it.

"I won't," she exclaimed. "I'm not going to do it!" She suddenly tried to jerk herself away, but as the girl clutched her with thighs and hands she fell forward instead. Her mouth pressed against the blonde's lovely cunt and the flame of her desire suddenly blazed up again. She covered the girl's whole sex with her mouth, and thrust her darting tongue into it as far as she could reach.

"You deceitful thing, you," the girl cried. "You knew that I couldn't make you stop once you had your tongue in my slit." She writhed and twisted, rubbing her cunt against Clara's mouth, and her hands tightened into fists. "But next time," she gasped, "next time you won't trick me like that. I'll make you kiss my ass. I'll make you beg on your knees to be allowed to do it. With tears in your eyes. See if I don't."

Her own arms were holding her legs up and open, pressing outward against the inside of her thighs, and both Clara's hands were crossed over her own sex, tickling herself as she kissed and tongued the other girl. She was close to coming, and she sucked wildly at the girl's open cunt the while she was caressing her own sex and pressed a searching forefinger onto her swollen clitoris.

Suddenly the other girl arched her back and quivered violently, her muscles taut and her hands clenched in Clara's hair, straining her head down into the flooding slit that was begging for her kisses. She came . . . and came . . . and then collapsed on the couch, her legs relaxed and wide apart, permitting and even inviting Clara to satisfy her own desires in any way she saw fit.

Clara's fingers fluttered feverishly in her own sex, as she rolled her tongue deep inside the girl's slit, and her own emotions grew hotter moment by moment. She was breathing in short gasps that ruffled the hair on the girl's muff, her whole body was tensed in a surge of passion and desire. She was taut, she was coming . . . coming . . . coming. The room whirled around and around. A blaze of light seemed to dazzle her eyes. She imagined that she was being possessed by fantastically stalwart lovers, one after another. She thought that in another moment she would die . . . and then it was all over.

The lights in the theater came on, and Clara sat

up . . . drawing her dress together to conceal her naked breasts, and fluffing her hair into some semblance of order. She hoped that no one was looking attentively at her, for she felt sure that if so they would guess what she had been doing. It must be written on her face, she told herself, and blushed scarlet at the remembrance.

Clara turned to the girl, and noticed that her eyes were still closed, and that she had not realized that the lights were turned on again. She reached forward quickly to pull down the girl's dress and hide her nakedness before it was noticed by the other people in the theater, and then suddenly she half faltered and drew back as though she had been struck. For on the girl's belly, in exactly the same spot that Clara remembered on Alice Burton, was the unmistakable red brand of the fatal Scorpion.

Clara could hardly have been more frightened if the scorpion had been real, and she pressed her hand tremblingly to her mouth to smother an exclamation of dismay. Then she recalled the lights and gingerly drew the girl's dress down over her bare thighs. She open her eyes at this movement and sat up and began to adjust her clothing herself.

"Are you staying?" the girl asked. "I think I'll go and see if my friend has arrived yet."

"I'm going too," said Clara, "I don't want to see any more just now." They walked down the corridor and were halfway to the hall when Clara essayed a tentative question. "I see the Scorpion bit you too," she remarked with a little sort of laugh, which even to her own ears didn't ring true. The girl stopped short in her tracks.

"What did you say?" she demanded.

"I just said that I noticed that you had one too," Clara replied, trying to sound casual.

"Just a minute," the girl said quickly. She stopped in front of Clara, raising her skirt and pulling down her panties a few inches at the waist. Then she let the dress drop again and said, "I didn't think so . . ." looking hard at Clara.

"Oh! I didn't mean that I had one," Clara hurried to explain. "I only saw Mrs. Burton's." She smiled uncertainly and waited for the other girl to say something more, but she was silent. So she too remained silent, and they parted at the foot of the stairs.

"I'm Bess Lynd," said the girl, "and I already know who you are. So shall we meet for a swim tomorrow morning?" And with a smile and a nod she vanished upstairs, leaving Clara prey to new curiosities and fears.

There was no sign of the D.A. anywhere, nor of Alice Burton, so Clara decided that she too might be better in bed. She undressed quickly, her mind intent on her discoveries that evening, and she had almost forgotten her own problems until she caught sight of her naked reflection in the mirror. Then all her past shame came rushing back. She saw herself in the mirror as a stranger . . . a stranger with unknown, devious ways and impulses.

She studied the stranger's face. She could see nothing there hinting of the depravity which she felt must be there, waiting to whisper the lewd thoughts which still floated around like dim ghosts in her mind. She touched her firmly rounded breasts, and the nipples prickled as she did so. She remembered what the girl had told her to do with the perfume, and she sniffed at them. There was a faint odor of Bess Lynd's sex, a hint of passion and desire. Clara blushed and fled into the bathroom. Guiltily she took a perfume bottle from her dressing table and drew the glass stopper across her pink nipples. It stung them a little. She must have skinned them, she thought, when she . . . she tried very hurriedly not to complete the image and hastily jumped into bed.

As she lay there wiggling her bare toes against the cool sheets, her memory took her back through the events of the day, try as she would to shut them out. Embraces-passion-desire . . . desire-passion-embraces, a never ending chain in a scenic sequence. "Don't let me remember tomorrow how much I liked watching it," she whispered into her pillow, "and don't ever let me go back there again."

Restless and unable to sleep, she picked up a book on the bedside table and began to read:—

"Please be seated, Reverend Father," said the Prioress. "I shall send for the two novices immediately." She rang the bell on her desk as she spoke, and very shortly after there was a knock on the door and two nuns entered, bringing the culprits with them.

Sister Dorothy was tall and slender, but her religious garb hid her figure, and her coif covered so much of her hair and part of her face that little was discernible with the exception of a somewhat full-lipped mouth and a pair of darkly passionate eyes.

Sister Frances was similarly attired, but she was not quite so tall, and even her novice's gown failed to disguise entirely the feminine curves of her bosom and hips.

Having conducted their charges thus far the nuns bowed slightly to the Father and withdrew, leaving the two girls standing hesitantly before the Prioress' desk. Taking not the slightest notice of their presence the Prioress turned to Father Anthony and addressed him as though they were alone in the room.

"Sisters Dorothy and Frances set a very bad example to the other novices," she said with a frown. "They whisper and plan together in corners of the garden, and even visit each other's cells at night, to the great scandal of the convent. I therefore decided to take advantage of your visit, Reverend Father, and have them brought before us for examination and punishment!"

"I am fully in agreement with your decision, Reverend Mother," replied Father Anthony. "It seems that the question to be decided is how serious were their faults and what sort of punishment have they deserved?"

"Two nights ago," replied the Prioress, "I was wakened by the Sister in charge of the novices, who asked me to come with her to Sister Frances' cell in order that I might observe what was happening there.

"Opening the door very quietly we entered without our presence being noticed, and discovered to our horror that not only were these two Sisters lying naked on the bed engaged in amorous embraces, but that two other novices were also present and encouraging them to further excesses."

"But what was actually occurring when you entered?" inquired Father Anthony, shaking his head gravely.

"I hardly know how to describe it to you," murmured the Prioress, averting her eyes as she spoke. "Both the other novices were completely naked, their gowns tossed on the cell floor, while Sister Frances was lying on her back on the bed with her legs wide apart and everything fully exposed. Sister Dorothy was stooping above her while one of the novices teased her breasts and the other felt between her thighs and fingered her slit.

"Then while we watched, she let herself fall forward so that she lay full length between Sister Frances' thighs, and with amorous movements began to rub their sexes together. In a few moments their passionate kisses and the convulsive quick jerkings of their bodies showed us what was about to take place, and the two younger novices ceased their provocative caresses and clung to each other in an ardent embrace, their hands busily occupied between each other's legs.

"At this point we made our presence known, and ordered the culprits to dress and return to their respective cells until their punishment had been decided on."

During this recital of girlish misdemeanors, Father Anthony's face had reddened with excitement, and he watched with interest Sister Dorothy's blushingly averted countenance. At the conclusion he shook his head as if astonished, and then said: "Your account of these misdeeds is really shocking, Reverend Mother, and I feel that any punishment which you may decide to inflict will be well merited."

Rising to her feet the Prioress emerged from behind her desk, and regarding the trembling and apprehensive novices with severity, said in a stern voice: "I have considered the matter most carefully, Reverend Father, and I have decided that the two Sisters shall undress themselves and be whipped naked in your presence, indeed, if you wish, you may inflict the punishment with your own hands. Now, Sister Dorothy, Sister Frances, remove your gowns and prepare yourselves for the whip at once."

The two shrinking and terrified girls fell on their knees and stretched out imploring hands to her as she spoke. "Ohh! No! Reverend Mother!" they cried. "Not naked before a man!! Whip us yourself in our own cells, but don't make us expose ourselves to Father Anthony! We shall die of shame!"

The Prioress took no notice of their pleas. "I do not intend to discuss the matter further," she said firmly, "so remove all your clothing immediately and stand here before me completely naked."

Sister Dorothy was the first to obey her command. With trembling fingers she loosened the cord belted around her waist and began to remove her gown. As it parted down the front all her naked bosom was exposed, showing two tempting pink-tipped breasts. The coarse clothing slid from her shoulders, revealing all her girlish body, nude except for a pair of plain linen drawers. She proceeded to remove these next, slipping them over her hips and down her rounded thighs to her feet, which in their turn were bared as she kicked off a pair of rope sandals.

In the meantime Sister Frances had also disrobed,

ana the two girls stood there naked side by side, with all their youthful charms fully displayed. Dorothy had removed her coif and allowed her hair to fall in curling confusion over her soft bosom, which it half concealed. Her girlish body was adorable, with its slender waist and rounded thighs, between which a tiny pink slit showed among a cluster of dark curls.

On the other hand, Frances' close-cropped hair would have made her appear almost boyish if it had not been for her twin breasts with their pouting nipples. A bush of reddish curls partly hid the line of her sex, and extended thence in downy wisps half-way to her navel.

Father Anthony, meanwhile, had obtained a whip from the desk, and now approached them from behind, holding it firmly in his hand.

"Just a moment," exclaimed the Prioress, with a gesture of restraint. "Don't you think, Reverend Father, that you will need more freedom of movement than your robe allows? I really think you should permit me to remove it for you." And suiting the action to the word, she loosened his girdle and raised the skirts of his gown sufficiently to prove that he wore nothing else underneath it.

"Oh! Oh! Father! For shame! What is this I see?" exclaimed the Prioress with a mocking laugh, as she relinquished her hold on his garment and with eager fingers brought into view as fine a weapon of love as any ever wielded in amorous combat by monk or layman.

"I fully realize now that there is no need of a whip for these dainty limbs when so pleasant an instrument of punishment is at hand," she remarked, as she fingered it with a loving touch and cast a glance sideways at the two novices, so as to observe their reactions to this new turn of events.

The two girls had remained where they were, naked and trembling, seemingly petrified with astonishment at what was taking place. Then they realized that it was a man's sex which was thus displayed before them, and that their own delightful nudity was effecting quite a notable increase in its size. They crimsoned with embarrassment and their blushes spread from face to bosom and thence to their slender bodies, until they turned away to conceal their complete confusion.

"Now, Father, if you sit on this stool and Frances kneels in front of you, with her head on your knees, you can whip her at your ease, while Dorothy kneels at the penitent's bench to await her turn."

And so saying, the Prioress thrust the shrinking girl to her knees on the stone floor before him.

The naked girlish body thus offered for punishment was so temptingly exposed, the rounded limbs so delicately white, that Father Anthony hesitated to begin her chastisement. His fingers caressed in turn her slender waist, her bare bottom, her trembling thighs, and then, throwing aside the whip, he commenced to spank her with the flat of his hand.

Under the force of his blows Frances could only maintain her position by resting her arms on the Father's bare thighs, and as she stooped forward she found her face was almost in contact with a masculine weapon of which she had often dreamed but which she had never before beheld. There was a fascination in the male sex odor and in the proud erection of the penis, which thrust stiffly toward her as if in attack, and jerked spasmodically in time with the blows which fell on her bare behind.

Almos⁺ unconsciously her shame at being whipped was giving place to another very different emotion, and her errant hand quitted his thigh and crept upward until her fingers discovered the Father's balls amidst the surrounding hair and commenced to gently squeeze and caress them. As she did this Frances bent forward still further, as if to facilitate her whipping, but in reality to enable her to brush her cheek very lightly against his sex. As it throbbed and swelled in response to her touch, her growing passion overcame her last traces of modesty. She twisted her head around until with moistly parted lips she could kiss the object of her desire. She touched it tentatively with her tongue, and then with uncontrollable ardor drew the swelling head right into her mouth.

At this moment, the Prioress, who had been watching the proceedings with great interest, thought it well to intervene. "I think that the rest of her punishment could wait now," she said, "and I am sure that Sister Dorothy must be almost frozen kneeling there with no clothes on. A little of your Fatherly attention would doubtless warm her up!"

At her mocking words Frances twisted free from Father Anthony's restraining hand and jerked her head back, blushing from head to foot in her confusion. As the surprised monk rose to his feet the Prioress pointed to the naked girl still on her knees at the penitent's bench across the room. Then she took his moist and rigid penis in her hand and softly fingered it up and down, and while continuing this exciting caress drew him into position behind the kneeling novice.

With her free hand the Prioress gently patted Dorothy's rounded buttocks, and with softly insistent fingers opened the way between the tempting mounds. Pointing the red tip at its delicious target she moved it to and fro in the yielding slit until Dorothy gave down an amorous dew which fully lubricated her virgin sex.

"Open your legs a little, Dorothy," she said, "and you, Father, push upward gently until you are all the way in her. While you, Frances, stand just here and slip your hand in from between his thighs and tickle both of them while he enters her."

Poor Dorothy, who had been kneeling on the cold stones all this time, and shiveringly anticipating a whipping on her tender behind, now found it invaded by a man's penis instead, warm and slippery and swelling, while its surrounding sex-hair tickled and excited her at the same time. She thought that this enormous prick could never penetrate her girlish slit, but she parted her thighs still more and the hot lips of her cunt yielded still further as her passions mounted, until she could feel the hot tip thrusting and searching at the mouth of her womb itself.

Her deliciously naked body was jerking and twisting in frantic passion at this amorous penetration, her buttocks and thighs opening and closing convulsively at each thrust, and inarticulate cries of desire issued from her panting lips. "OH! NO! Please stop! You're hurting me! You can't get it all in, I'm too small! Oh! Ohh! Please! Frances! Frances! Stop him, stop him!

No, don't! Tickle me in front! That's right! It's maddening to be felt like that! Now push! I'll open my legs more! Tickle him too, Frances! Make him come soon! Quick! I can't wait! Squeeze his balls! Ah! Ah! Now I can feel him coming! Take me! Take me! Ohhh! Ohhh! Ohhhhh!"

Chapter 12

When Clara opened her eyes next morning, she discovered the D.A. sitting at the foot of her bed. She was a little bit startled but she tried not to show it. "How long have you been here?" she inquired.

"This long," he replied, indicating the ash on his cigar. "I knocked on the door but there was no answer. Do you realize it's one-thirty already?"

Clara sat up and began to stretch, but had to clutch at the sheet hurriedly as it fell away and disclosed her pouting breasts. "Will you please hand me my negligee and look the other way?" she said to the D.A. as she shrank back and held the sheet ¹oser to her body.

Conrad crossed the room and lazily picked up her robe from the chair. "I think you'd better come and get it," he said as he paused just out of her reach. "Stop hiding yourself that way, you'll be smothered."

"Perhaps I prefer to smother rather than have you ogling my naked body?" Clara riposted. "Please give me my robe."

The D.A. apparently was impressed by her serious tone. "Very well . . . here you are," he murmured. He stepped forward toward the bed, but as Clara sat up and reached for the garment he dropped it and snatched the sheet away. Clara sat glaring furiously at him, but she made no further attempt to hide her nudity.

"Sometimes I just hate you," she said tensely. "You can be so nice when you want, but you so seldom do want."

The D.A. seated himself on the bed again. He caressed her bare shoulders, at the same time dilating his nostrils with an inquiring sniff. "What kind of perfume are you using?" Conrad asked. Clara felt the blood rush to her cheeks. She realized that her face was betraying her, and she was more angry with herself than with him. It was uncanny, she thought, how he invariably managed to find the one vulnerable spot in her own defenses against him.

The D.A. sniffed again and leaned toward her. Clara tried feebly to prevent him from touching her taut breasts. "Not musk " he said, "but very reminiscent." He pushed her protecting hands away and lowered his face to her nipples. He brushed them with his lips, very gently, sniffed again, and then made a thoughtful kind of sound in his throat.

"Please stop," said Clara. "Please go away and let me dress. It's so late!"

He patted her bare thigh and stood up. "I'll go and get ready for a swim," he said, "it's time you had a change of sport." When he was gone Clara sprang from the bed and threw her robe angrily to the floor and stamped on it. Then she went into the bathroom and sat down . . . to think!

Half an hour later she was in the swimming pool with a number of the other guests, some of whom she recognized from the previous day. She greeted one or two whom she knew, watched Conrad deep in jesting conversation with Bess Lynd, had a drink on the tiled veranda, and went back to her bedroom to shower and dress for a late lunch.

Clara was so startled that she cried "Ohh!" quite loudly. Then she turned off the shower and faced him. "That's twice today you've done that," she accused him angrily. "You've got to stop it. Besides I thought you were too busy talking to Bess to follow me upstairs."

Conrad spread his hands in a disclaiming gesture. "I did not intend to startle you," he said. "I called out, but the shower was making such a noise you didn't hear me. And then you looked so charming I didn't want to interrupt you. As for your Miss Lynd, I was merely trying to pump her about the Scorpion."

He offered Clara a cigarette, and she stuck her head out of the shower alcove to accept a light. He fingered her bathing suit, a mute question in his eyes.

"Oh, I was just washing it out on me," Clara said. "I took my real shower before we went down to the pool."

"Washing off your perfume?" he suggested slyly.

She flushed. "No," she said. "I always take a shower when I get up in the morning."

"Well, I haven't had mine yet," he said. "Do you mind if I take mine with you?"

"You mean . . . take a shower together?" Clara asked. It did seem a peculiar and possibly perverted form of intimacy. She hung back as he reached toward her shoulder strap.

"The water isn't hurting my suit," she said nervously.

"No, but your lack of enthusiasm is hurting me," he

166

told her. "A bath together would be still more fun, but that can wait." He put one arm about her waist and pulled her shoulder straps down. When the costume was far enough down to expose her breasts he bent and sniffed at her nipples once more. "You changed your perfume," he teased her.

Clara tried to push him away, but he stubbornly refused to be pushed. "This is the stupidest, most childish thing I ever heard of," she told him.

"Yes," he concurred, "but very economical too." He patted her shoulder gently. "Shall I take off your costume the rest of the way, or will you?" She did not reply, and so he continued to pull her suit down till it finally reached her hips. He tickled her navel, and when that made her squirm he took advantage of her movement to get the dress down to her knees.

"Really, you might as well take it off now, don't you think?" he queried. He nodded toward a tall mirror facing them from the back of the bathroom door, and Clara looked at their reflections in it. She thought she looked very indecent in her bright red bathing cap, and then nothing else except her mussed bathing suit tangled around her knees, her breasts bobbing and her bare behind sticking cheekily out back of her. Her naked belly was close to his, and her muff almost touched his leg.

"I'll . . . I'll take it off," she hesitated, choosing what she hoped was the lesser of two evils. "Don't hold me any more now, or I can't do it."

He released her, and she stepped out of the suit with a quick movement, turning her back to him as she did so. She dropped the suit outside the shower, and turned the water on quickly, hoping to be in and out of it before he could strip and follow her. But before the water had done more than wet her, he was in the spray too, as naked as she. She drew her shoulders back and stamped her bare feet with a little smacking sound. "Please pass me the soap," she said, in what she hoped was a matter of fact voice. Really, she thought, this was too absurd for anything, to be naked with a man in a shower and asking him to pass one the soap.

"The nicest part of taking a shower with somebody else is that you don't have to stand on your head trying to wash inaccessible spots," Conrad told her. He was working up a fine lather with his hands and shouting above the noise of the shower. When the soapsuds foamed up he reached out and pulled Clara from beneath the spray.

"But I don't mind at all taking my own shower," Clara exclaimed, as he began to soap her shoulders and arms. "I don't have any inaccessible places, truly I don't."

"And that's the truth," he jested, and Clara blushed as she realized the twisted meaning he had given her remark. By now great blobs of soapsuds were slithering down her rounded breasts and arms, and the slippery feeling of his hands on her soft skin vaguely reminded her of something else which she could not quite place. She tried to take the cake of soap from his hands but he shook his head. "You'll like it better as we progress," he told her. "You see if you don't." He covered her breasts with his hands and gently rubbed the soap across her taut nipples.

"My breasts don't need washing," Clara said, a little

surprised at how coolly she had called them by name.

"I don't believe I'd want to give a bath to a girl who really needed one," Conrad replied. He rubbed masses of lather into her armpits, until little beards of foam dripped down her flanks. He rotated his hands over her belly ever so gently, and Clara hardly noticed that he continued it in ever-increasing circles until he was soaping her delta and thighs as well, filling her muff with foam, making it look all straggly and, Clara thought, ridiculous. He slipped his fingers between her thighs and began to soap her slit. "And I certainly wouldn't want to do this if I thought it was really necessary," Conrad added.

He dropped to one knee and began rubbing Clara's calves and knees, reaching down to her ankles and feet. She looked down at herself, her sudsy breasts and belly, and his own wet nakedness. Suddenly he looked up and found her eyes on him. He dropped the soap and hugged her knees, rubbing his cheeks against her stomach and the dripping hair of her muff.

"Please get up," Clara said in some embarrassment. But he stayed where he was for a few more minutes. He worked his hands over the rounds of her buttocks and between them, and he soaped the small of her back, but he came back and reached in through her legs to lather her crotch, while his face remained pressed close to her thighs in front.

His fingers lingered over her cunt and bottom, and she began to feel curiously excited as to further developments. At last he got to his feet and lathered her between her smooth shoulders and down the small of her back, completing the task he had set himself. "Don't wash it off yet," he said, as she took a step toward the shower. "It's your turn to work on me now!" He gave her the soap, but Clara only shook her head.

"There's only one place that's hard to reach," she said, "I'll lather your back, but that's all."

"You'll wash me all over," Conrad said, taking her by the wrist and speaking in a determinedly gentle voice. "And you won't stop till I tell you to." He set her hands in motion on his chest, and soon had a lather worked up in the hairy patch between his nipples. Pretty soon Clara had been persuaded that she might as well continue on her own. She had never been aware of the contours of a man's body before, and after a few minutes her fingers began to seek them out and define them with caressing movements.

She rubbed his nipples, pretending not to notice that they hardened and stuck out just as hers did, though only in miniature, and a funny thrill seemed to shoot down her spine and curl in her bottom for a minute before it continued right down to her pink toes. She put her fist filled with foam into his armpits and ran her hands down his flanks to his hips. He moved suddenly and she realized he was ticklish. And having discovered that she began to scratch lightly down his sides with her nails, just to make him squirm. And then she began to soap his belly too.

It was firmer than she had realized, but it had a way of fitting its shape to her hands, so that it felt slightly rounded wherever she touched it. But with her hands so low on his body she found that she must, if she watched what she was doing, occasionally let her eyes drop to his hairy sex. It was like a root and two bulbs, she thought vaguely, but then the simile of planting came to her mind, and she felt all funny once more.

She discovered that the hair which she had thought grew only around his prick and in a delta above it, as hers did, in reality ran up quite high and nearly to his navel. She rubbed soap into the button there, tickling it gently with one slim finger.

"Are you going to soap my stomach the whole afternoon?" the D.A. queried, and she realized that she had been going over and over the same region for several minutes. He took her wrist and guided her hand down. "Try it here instead if you want to kill time," he suggested.

Clara closed her fingers over his prick with a softly caressing touch, feeling very tender toward it because for the moment it was so soft and small and so strangely outside her previous experience of it. She gently squeezed his sex, and the suds oozed up between her fingers. Not quite realizing what she was doing, since it was the only way of handling a prick in her adult experience, she began softly moving her hand up and down along the shaft. A change came over the organ and once more it was familiar to her. Her fingers sensed the change as it took place, its slow growth, and a new excitement began to mount in her as it slowly developed. She felt strange and in a way elated and subtly flattered as Conrad's prick filled her hand.

She rubbed handfuls of soapy foam into his hairy delta and then covered his balls with a creamy lather. And steadily, as she rolled his testicles between her soft palms, his cock just above them kept swelling and thrusting proudly upward. And Clara had a curious satisfaction in it as she realized it was the touch of her hands that was achieving this.

Suddenly she realized that she had spent many minutes soaping his crotch and sex, minutes during which neither had said a word, and her shameless femininity escaped her and she was terribly abashed once more. She drew her hands away and looked up to find the D.A. was again smiling down at her. A warm glow seemed to invade Clara's temples and cheeks and spread right down to her bosom, and she turned her face away to hide her blushes.

"You'll have to kneel down to do my legs," he remarked. And Clara suddenly found herself on her knees without knowing how she got there. She was running her soapy fingers around his ankles and between his legs and up his thighs. He pulled her to him by her hair, and pressed his rampant virility up into the groove between her breasts.

"Press your breasts together," he told her softly. She looked up at him with big eyes.

"Is this part of taking a shower together?" she asked.

"Please, darling," he said in a low voice.

"Darling!" He had said "Darling!" Had he ever said it to her before? She was sure he hadn't. Her breasts ached and felt heavy and her throat choked up. She suddenly realized she was in love with him Madly! She thought she was going to cry. She was still looking up at him, and his smiling eyes seemed very kind all of a sudden. Did he like her, she wondered? He must surely, or he wouldn't bother about her when there were so many more attractive and certainly more willing women waiting to submit to his desires.

Clara snapped out of her daydream and lifted her breasts together with both hands, pressing them around his rigid cock. He pushed up and down with his hips while she tickled the tip of his prick with her hardening nipples, the soapy foam sliding it easily between her swelling breasts.

Conrad realized that she had better stop, and he pushed her gently away with his hands, turning around so as to look at her over his shoulders. She covered the back of his thighs with soap and then ran her hands over his buttocks. Between his legs she could see his balls and the lather-dripping hair, and she could see the hair at the back too, where she had not washed him yet. She began to get to her feet.

"Wait," said the D.A. "Haven't you missed something?" He turned around to face her again, and she ran her hands in between his legs, soaping the whole of his crotch. Strange she thought, I don't feel ashamed any more. She kept rubbing him there until he pulled her to her feet. She lathered his back while facing him, passing her arms around his waist. He passed his stomach soapily across hers. His cock crossed her thighs, bouncing each time it was freed at one side or the other, and splattering suds from its tip. Clara felt her nipples straining in tight erection as they were pressed by his chest.

"Don't you think it's fun to take showers together?" he asked her. "I think it's lots of fun, darling."

He had said it again. Clara felt her body becoming all weak and yielding against his, but she was unable to restrain it. She didn't want to keep herself from leaning against him, but what had made her feel so weak, she wondered. Her arms and legs seemed for a moment to be as light as feathers, but when she experimentally willed herself to move away from his body they immediately became as heavy as lead. His knee was pushed between hers, and she felt the caress of his thigh as it gently spread her slit wide open. She leaned closer to the caress, but her voice protested. "We're doing more than taking a shower," she whispered. "You shouldn't do this to me."

His prick, terribly hard and upright, pressed into her belly, and he rubbed it there. The cake of soap was still in her hands, and she let it fall to the tiled floor and grasped his sex with both hands without a word or gesture of restraint. She pushed her fingers slowly up and down, curling them in his hair and around his prick, until there was a great ball of foam at his crotch, half-hiding the very movements that were now creating it. Then Conrad took a handful of foam from his groin and slipped his fingers into Clara's slit, covering her cunt with white bubbles. "Does it sting?" he asked, while he spread the lips of her cunt apart and squeezed the lather up between their soft folds.

"No! Yes . . . Just a tiny bit," Clara said. "It feels so slippery." She felt that she should be blushing and ashamed for having spoken so intimately of her cunt, but she wasn't. "I love him! I love him!" she kept on saying to herself, and she pressed her thighs closer together on his hand.

He was facing her squarely now, bending his knees a little and lowering the tip of his prick until it slowly pressed into her muff. It slipped in between her thighs, and Clara bit her lips to keep from crying out with

174

desire as its warm rigidity passed to and fro across her cunt. Its tip pressed so hard on her lips for a moment that she thought it would find entrance there, even though nothing more indiscreet than a questing forefinger had ever done so before.

And then Conrad drew away. He rubbed his cock just once or twice lightly across her yielding slit, and then stepped back and drew her with him beneath the shower. He turned the water full on for a moment, first hot and then cold. She felt terribly weak at the knees as he pulled her out and began to rub her down with an enormous bath towel. He patted her gently all over and then towelled her softly, front and back, until she began to glow. Then he dried himself. And Clara stood there without volition when he had finished, as if she had lost all power to move.

"Go into the bedroom and wait for me there," Conrad said. "Lie on the bed and wait for me." He fumbled with her hair and fluffed it out into damp masses. And Clara walked out of the shower like someone hypnotized. She was lying face down on the bed when she heard his almost noiseless step beside her. Gently he turned her over and raised her head on the pillows, exposing the full length of her slender naked body against the white sheets.

"Would you like to kiss me first?" he inquired, stroking her breasts and plucking softly at her pink nipples.

"First?" she whispered, as her eyes fluttered open and seemed to plead with him. "First?"

"This is where we carry our caresses to their logical conclusion," he replied. He knelt on the bed near her

175

shoulders and then straddled her breasts. His prick seemed smaller, but only slightly so, than before. Clara ran her fingers lightly along it and could feel it throb and harden. She closed her eyes, for by doing so she felt that she might shut it out, but the sight still remained with her. So she opened them again, and moved her head so that her mouth was a little nearer to its goal.

Clara did not quite know when her tongue reached out a pink tip and licked the tip of his cock. The D.A. leaned close and she maneuvered her tongue in a twisting caress that passed around the prick from one end to the other. It returned along the under surface until her mouth was at the tip again. A tiny sound, hardly a cry, came from deep in her throat, and she suddenly took the red bud in her lips. She sucked it in, and it grew and grew until her mouth was crammed with its warmth and she felt it must knock against the back of her throat. She put her hands against Conrad's body and pushed him away.

"I didn't ask you to do that, you know," he said softly, as she covered her face with her hands.

"I know you didn't," she exclaimed. "I did it because I knew you'd like me to, even if you didn't say so."

"And do you really want to do the things that I like?" he asked. He took her face in his hands, drawing her fingers away so that he could see her better. She was crying, but she was happy, and it suddenly seemed to her that this was the time to tell him her secret.

"Sometimes," she whispered, "when you are nice . . .

when you make me feel the way I do now . . . I want to do anything that you'd like."

"And how do you feel now?" he inquired.

Clara hesitated, and then took the plunge, wondering whether she should have waited for him to speak first. "I love you," she whispered very softly.

His face lit up, but he shook his head slowly. "You shouldn't," he replied. "I only make people unhappy."

Clara was radiant now. "I expect to be unhappy," she said. "Love always makes one unhappy, I think." She couldn't remember where she had heard that before, but she was sure it was true. True and unimportant at the same time. Suddenly the realization of her position at the moment flooded over her.

Here she was, lying under the thighs of a man who was straddling her breasts, his prick only inches from her mouth. And this was the situation in which she had chosen to tell him that she loved him. She felt a flush of shame flood right through her body, and then it was replaced by a sudden urge to forget anything and everything in his arms, to lose herself in him . . . this very instant.

Her thighs quivered. Her pink-tipped breasts swelled and throbbed. "I'll make you love me too," she told him. "Just see if I don't." And she raised her slim arms and twined them around his neck, pulling him down to her once more. She took his prick in her warm lips again, nibbling on it, teasing its tip with her tongue, sucking at it with all the sensuous desire that was possessing her.

"If you really mean . . ." Conrad began. And then

his voice trailed off, and his hips moved to and fro in a frantic embrace that kept them both speechless. Clara rolled her head from side to side as he fucked in and out of her mouth, tonguing the hot tip every time he drew it out, and sucking strongly every time he thrust it in. He realized very well that she had had no other teacher, and he was amazed that she could instinctively perform the act of love with such understanding. Even the cleverest of men cannot comprehend the possibilities of a girl in love.

Clara was sucking him in a perfect frenzy, throwing her head to and fro and banging it up and down on the pillow. He rested his hands behind her neck and leaned in to her, feeling her lips grow warmer and more amorous every moment. He knew he would spend in another moment . . . and that nothing could stop him now. He thought vaguely that it was a good idea to come once in her mouth before really fucking her, then he'd be sure to hold out for a long time when he was in her cunt. And then he forgot that and everything else too . . . as passion overcame him.

"Squeeze my balls," he told her. She did as she was bid . . . enthusiastically. "And . . . put one finger in at the back," Conrad continued, his voice tight with desire. She sucked and sucked, her eyes tightly shut and her hands caressing all his sex. He asked her again, coaxingly. "I'm coming in just about a second, darling. Please put one finger in, just there." He guided her hand between the cheeks of his bottom, but she drew it away. Then in a moment it was back again, wetted from her own dripping sex. The long index finger slid in and in, and Clara moved it to and fro as she sucked ecstatically on his throbbing prick.

Conrad gasped and jerked convulsively, almost falling across her face, and Clara found her mouth suddenly inundated with his jetting sperm. It was hot and salty and she swallowed with difficulty and a sense of shame, and then suddenly she was swallowing again, passionately, and wanting to. The prick gradually got small in her mouth, and she ran the tip of her tongue tenderly over its head, and then pushed it out. Her lips were swollen with passion, and wet with spend, and she licked them tentatively to gather in the last drops of his love juice.

Conrad rolled over on his side and lay there, relaxed and expended. Clara regarded him a little shyly. There was one drop forming on the tip of his softened cock, and suddenly desire welled up in her again and she reached out her mouth and took it on her tongue, rubbing it around on her lips as she opened and closed them.

Time passed, and Clara cuddled her cheek close to her man's thighs, idly fingering his sex. It began to rise again, and she kissed its swelling tip, leaning over to flutter her eyelashes against it. "You darling," said her man's voice, coming to her from ever so far away.

And then he took the initiative. He passed his hand down between her thighs and Clara felt that her cunt almost reached for his fingers. "You are wet, aren't you?" whispered Conrad, and she realized that her sex was simply dripping and that her thighs were sopping wet all the way down.

"Are you going to . . . to . . . fuck me now?" asked Clara in a tiny voice.

"Do you want me to?" he queried.

"Oh! Yes!" she cried softly. "Oh! Yes! What am I . . . what am I living for except to be loved? Don't you even love me just a little bit?" she added inconsequentially, as he made no reply to her passionate declaration.

"Yes! I love you," said Conrad suddenly. His voice was sincere and thrilled Clara through and through. Her sex wetted to overflowing, and all her body lifted to his male embrace. He pressed against her with his whole length and his prick thrust in and out between her thighs, driving her almost crazy with desire. He parted her legs and pressed in between them, while Clara held her breath and it seemed as if her heart must stop beating. He pressed his cock against the lips of her slit and she thought she would faint. This was tne moment of her life. She was a girl now . . . in another minute she would be a woman, a woman in love.

He made Clara put her hands between her legs and hold his prick while he passed it up and down in the moist lips of her cunt. Then he made her continue the embrace by moving her own hips up and down. He pulled her legs upward and planted her feet firmly on the bed beside his hips. She grasped his prick firmly and held the tip against the entrance to paradise pressing herself upward to him. Time after time she was at the point of pulling his prick deep within her, but each time he stopped just when she was a hair's breadth from ravishment.

"It will hurt if we are in too much of a hurry," he told her, and gently caressed her breasts.

"Ohh! Let it hurt me!" she gasped, "Only do it now!" and her eyes pleaded with him mutely.

But he only took her hands and laid her arms back of her head. Then he slid his arms under her knees and raised them till her feet were off the bed and her thighs were spread to their utmost. At last she was fully exposed to his attack, and he began to press his prick into her once more. She gave a sudden gasp and squirmed madly as he bore down on her with all his weight, telling her to lie still.

"But I can't lie still," she pleaded, noting how high her straining thighs were forced, and suddenly crossing her feet around his loins to press him closer to her. "I just can't lie still when you are doing this to me."

"If you keep still it will be over in a moment now, and it won't hurt you so much. You want to remember this as being something wonderful and thrilling, not as something that hurt you!" Conrad's voice died away, and he once more thrust deeply between the dripping lips of her slit.

Clara tried to stop squirming. It was an agony to do so, but somehow she managed to keep her muscles under control, although her body kept quivering uncontrollably. She felt she was experiencing that breathless moment when a circus audience waits for the leap from one high trapeze to the other. A drum seemed to beat in her head, and suddenly there was the shrill crashing climax of the cymbals. But there were no cymbals, she realized. It was her own voice, screaming her pain and delight as Conrad plunged into her.

She was happy now, and yet the strain seemed to be almost unbearable. The lips of her cunt were forced open to the point where something must yield. Her buttocks felt warm and sticky. Perhaps that was blood, she thought, and realized that she was right. Then she understood that her man had finally and forever possessed her, and that there was no reality to her own ownership of herself any more.

"I love you so," she whispered in his ear. "Tell me what to do next!"

Conrad showed her how to keep her knees raised, and how to pass her arms around his body. "You will know what else to do," he said, and began thrusting in and out of her, while Clara clung to him in a heatedly awkward embrace.

The touch of his sex burned in her like fire, but delight thrilled there too, and she lifted her hips to accept more of it. Her errors soon showed her how to rise against his stroke and fall when he withdrew, keeping him in her body motionless when she could stand no more. Her legs loosened their grip and fell all open on the pillow beneath her. He drove in and out unchallenged, and he lifted his face from where he had buried it on her shoulder, and clamped his mouth on hers, seeking her tongue with the tip of his. She pulled away from him to breathe. Utter confusion possessed her and she felt that she was swelling and about to burst.

"Don't stop!" she whispered. "Please don't . . stop!"

He pressed closer to her yielding body, and her hands moved vaguely along the small of his back as he raked in and out of her. Her hips rose in a tight arch against him. Another stroke, and another, and another. They were quivering in keen and mutual ecstasy. She gazed deep into his eyes as she felt his sperm jetting into her womb. And then she screamed again on a high note, for what had happened to her had never, never happened to her before. Never so deep inside her, and boiling through her whole yielding body to her heart's core.

Chapter 13

C lara turned over on the bed and opened her eyes as a hand gently shook her by the arm. It was Alice Burton.

"I didn't mean to startle you," she said with a hesitant smile, "but Conrad asked me to give you a message."

Clara bit her lip on hearing the other woman use the D.A.'s first name so casually, but she managed to smile. Alice studied the smile for a moment, and then said, "Aren't we to be friends any more?"

"I don't know," said Clara doubtfully. "I don't know if I'm clever enough to remain friends with you."

Alice Burton hesitated for a minute. "But I just wanted to go to bed with him," she said. "And nothing more. I promise you I've done nothing to alter your position with him." She looked down at Clara's pouting breasts, so openly attracted that Clara felt a little surge of satisfied vanity. "I really did come with a message," she continued. "Conrad asked me to find you and ask if you would please join him in his room as soon as possible. So you see how much you have to fear from me after all!"

"I'm so glad!" Clara breathed. "Because you see . . I love him. And I only realized it yesterday."

She made her way down the corridor to Conrad's room, her cheeks tingling with Alice's parting kiss. How was it possible, she wondered, to love a man and be attracted to a woman at the same time. Whatever it was that she felt . . . and she was not sure what it was, it was apparent in her face when the D.A. opened his door in answer to her knock, for he stared intently at her.

"Alice Burton is a remarkably versatile woman," he said in a tone which brought blushes flooding to Clara's face again. "But that doesn't concern us at present," he added. "I found out something which might have a bearing on your sister's whereabouts perhaps, so if you want to come along we had better get moving."

He took a package from a drawer and slipped it into his pocket, as he led her from the room and down the corridor once more. "There's a meeting of some of the people here in a few minutes," he said. "There may be a Black Mass or something of that sort, and perhaps the Scorpion might put in there by some chance or other."

"What's a Black Mass?" Clara asked.

He told her, and she looked at him in amazement. The whole idea was so bizarre that it staggered her. The black candle and the goat, the blonde virgin, the consecrated and desecrated Host, the cross upside down and spat upon, the Paternoster recited backwards. It seemed crazily impossible. She gulped and said hesitantly, "Well . . . if you think we might find Rita . . . or something . . ."

They passed on down the hall, and Clara clung to his arm as they left behind the room where she had been switched, the big bedroom where she had seen the girl in the sweater beaten, and then her own room of so many memories. At the end of a second hall they entered a dark antechamber with a strange heavy scent

185

pervading it. And in the large room which they entered next, the light from the blue lanterns hanging in the corners was so dim that for a few moments she could discern nothing at all.

Then she discovered that the walls of the room were high and covered with mirrors where one would expect to find windows. And that cushions were strewn about the floor in heaped confusion. Conrad pulled her down beside him in one corner and settled her comfortably on them. Next he picked up two pipes lying on a table near by, and took from his pocket the package which Clara now realized was the little silver box which she had originally found in her sister's drawer.

She caught her breath. "Oh!" she said. "Are we . . . are we going to smoke it?" She felt suddenly afraid of the unknown. "Is that what the other people are smoking and smiling over?"

"Yes!" replied Conrad. "We are . . . and it is!" He handed her a small pipe already filled. "Draw deeply on it," he said to her as he turned to fill his own pipe.

She puffed at it for a few minutes, and nothing seemed to happen. She took half a dozen more puffs, deeper this time. And then she suddenly felt dizzy, as if she were going around in circles. How queer to go around in circles, she thought, and giggled suddenly and hurriedly put her hand over her mouth to check it.

"I'm thirsty," she whispered to Conrad, and reached for his hand, in which there had miraculously appeared a tall glass. She seemed to be drinking quarts and quarts, taking days in the process. But Conrad was still sitting in the same place when she finished. "Why did you give me lemonade?" she asked. "Did I want lemonade?"

"That was wine," the D.A. said. "How do you feel?"

"I don't know, I never felt this way before," Clara replied. And then forgot both question and answer.

There was a girl across the room from her, she noticed. She was sprawled on a pile of cushions just as Clara was, and there was one man on the floor beside her and another sitting in a chair by her side. Her hand was in the lap of the man in the chair, and she was caressing him sensuously. The man down on the floor with her was slowly running his hand up and down her thigh, raising her dress each time a little further, and never lowering it to where it had been.

"Watch them," Clara whispered to the D.A. and then she blushed crimson at having said it. She felt that she, like all those others in the room, was just governed by the one desire.

She turned her eyes back to the girl after an interval of what seemed hours and hours. The girl was unbuttoning the trousers of the man on the chair, and the other man was now caressing her hips, which were completely naked by this time. An excitement which Clara could hardly endure seemed to run from somewhere in her brain and down her back to her loins, whence it radiated out until it possessed her whole body. And especially her cunt, which felt so flooded already that she was sure she was going to float away. She buried her fists in the pillows, pressing her lips tightly together lest she cry out to the girl across the room.

The girl took out the prick of the man in the chair. She began to stroke it caressingly, and then she clasped her fingers tightly around it and moved them up and

187

down. Her hand was signaling in Morse, so much Clara understood, but she thought it was in Scandinavian, and she could not translate it.

The girl turned her hips, letting the man on the floor pull her dress way above her waist. She was wearing nothing underneath, and her bare buttocks shone whitely across the room as the man petted her behind. It was like a full moon in its loveliness. I suppose I will be unwell next week, thought Clara crazily, trying not to laugh aloud.

"Take off my dress, Fred!" the girl's voice sang in the silence and rang in Clara's ears. "Let them all see me with my dress off." And she leaned back for him to take it off over her head, but put his hand aside while she reached for her silk stockings. She rubbed her hands down from her shoulders slowly, caressingly, passing them over her belly to her thighs. Then she pressed them on her slit, twining her fingers sensuously in the sex-hair and opening and closing her knees slowly, again and again, and displaying her cunt to everybody in the room. And especially to me, thought Clara.

Clara felt her own crotch tingle, and she thought of her own hair growing secretly between her legs. She felt as if they all had separate identities of their own, and when she moved her legs slightly she could feel how each individual one curled. She became unbearably aware of her own cunt. The lips were squeezed together, and as she realized this she spread her legs to liberate them, and they parted like reluctant lovers, with a soft kiss

The naked girl across the room turned toward the man in the chair, facing him on her knees. She shook her head and her hair fell over her face like rain. Rubbing and handling the man's prick, she pressed herself in between his knees and leaned toward him. Her lips faltered near his cock, dipped and then hesitated. The man stroked her smooth white shoulders and then passed his hands under her armpits as he leaned forward. He squeezed her breasts, and the girl suddenly pulled his prick to her lips and sucked it right into her mouth.

Clara gasped and thought that she herself must choke. She glanced sideways at Conrad, but his expression disclosed little of what his thoughts might be. She looked back across the room once more.

The girl was sucking the man's sex as though she wished to draw it from his body. Her head twisted from side to side, and it seemed to Clara that the rampant organ must drive right down her throat. She flung her body wildly about, clinging to the man's knees, and then thrust him away as she collapsed on the floor, swallowing heavily and licking at her flooded lips.

Clara took a deep breath, for she felt stifled. Her own body was so overwrought that even the touch of her clothes was an agony to her.

The girl was on her knees now, with her breasts very nearly touching the floor. Her buttocks shone whitely in the dim light, inviting an intimate caress. The girl was swinging her breasts now, letting them touch the rug, trembling at its roughness, while her hair fell in wild confusion over her face. Clara squirmed, "No! No!" she whispered. "I can't bear it!" And she crossed her hands across her own breasts, caressing the nipples

189

to soothe away the hurt from the rug which she had felt as she watched the other girl.

The man's prick was touching the girl's behind now, sliding over her buttocks and pressing in between them. The girl's head jerked up sharply and her back arched tensely. She clenched her hands as the rampant cock rubbed across the lips of her cunt.

"Not there!" she whispered frantically. "Not in my cunt." Her voice was aching with desire. "You know where I like it," she gasped. She spread her legs in a way that seemed to open her buttocks more, and took the man's prick in her hand again. She pressed it up and down in the slit of her cunt and then along the crease of her white behind. A soft moan came from her lips. "There!" she panted. "In there!"

Clara's mind soared. She was in a Persian garden, and naked girls were fanning her with palm leaves while a little negro boy was tickling her between the legs with a peacock's feather. She turned restlessly on the cushions. Where was the sultan, her lord and master? When would he come and cleave the split fig running with sap between her thighs? Her mind was whirling around. And then she was back in the darkened room beside Conrad, and neither of them had stirred.

The naked girl across the room spoke again. "There!" she whispered as she had whispered before. And Clara realized that space and time had altered meanings now The girl was still caressing the man's prick in her hand, its swollen tip was still probing between her tempting buttocks in the curling hair that half concealed the desired entrance. Clara tightened her own buttocks involuntarily against that thrusting prick and she felt her cunt lips and the cheeks of her behind squeeze protectively together. She felt recklessly lustful and at the same time frightened by shame. She loved Conrad, and yet she trembled as she felt his hands on hers. She let herself be drawn to him. His arms went around her waist and he ran his finger along the groove of her botton.

"It could just as well be you, couldn't it?" he said, as he prolonged the caress in what seemed to Clara the most indecent manner.

"What does . . . how do you mean?" Clara faltered. "What could just as well be me?" she added, and all his hundreds of fingers seemed to be caressing her bottom silkily.

"I don't have to tell you," he murmured. "You know very well!" And Clara did know . . . all too well. She looked again at the girl while Conrad raised her own skirt along her thigh. The girl on the rug was so excited that it was terrifying to watch her. The D.A. pulled Clara's dress up to her hips and leaned close to her, whispering "I want you to take off your panties for me."

"Not now!" Clara exclaimed, her heart pounding until it filled her breasts. "We'll go back to my room!"

"Take them off," he insisted, "or I'll make you lie down and I'll take them off myself in front of every body."

Clara slipped her hand under his as his fingers moved quickly down her hip. She took the waistband of her panties and slid them down an inch. "I can't," she pleaded, "don't make me take them off here!" But his hand tightened over her wrist and hurt, as he forced her to pull her panties down yards and yards . . . a whole three inches in fact.

"Wait!" she whispered. "Wait until no one is looking." She reached under her dress on the other side and lifted her hips. Very cautiously she drew her panties down over her soft buttocks. Inch by inch she wiggled them down to her knees. Then she drew her legs under her and slipped the panties right off and away, burying them under a cushion with one quick movement. Although she was still covered by her dress, she felt entirely naked with nothing on from her waist down, and she shivered with shame and eager anticipation.

"What are you going to do?" she asked in a trembling whisper. "Please tell me what you are going to do to me?"

"Watch!" said Conrad, nodding toward the naked girl.

The man was bending closer to her, both hands placed caressingly on her rounded buttocks. His fingers slipped down the back of her thighs to her knees, then up between her soft thighs once more to her cunt. He slipped a finger into her slit, twisting it around while he pressed his prick into her other aperture. It was penetrating further and further between her buttocks, and it seemed to Clara that it must already be entering the girl's body and her own as well. She seemed to be the girl as well as herself.

"No, he mustn't do it!" Clara protested. "No! I don't want it to happen!"

"To you or to her?" the D.A. asked. He ran his fingers meaningly along the small of her back and lightly stroked her behind. He felt her buttocks and hugged her closer, so that her hips were slightly raised. Then he slipped his hand under her and tickled the tender parts of her thighs.

"It's too real," Clara pleaded. "It's exactly as if it were happening to me . . ."

"Yes . . . and it is happening to you . . . if you let it," the D.A.'s voice reached her through a haze. His fingers slid into her crotch, rubbing her hair apart and tickling her yielding cunt. He pressed the lips together to spread the wetness well over them, then he parted them again by running his middle finger along the crack. He plucked at her clitoris until she was all on fire, and then quite suddenly he plunged his hand deeply into her feverish cunt.

Clara covered her mouth and bit her knuckle to stop from screaming, for just at the moment when Conrad's finger had stabbed into her, the man across the room had unexpectedly driven his prick into the naked girl's cunt. The short soft cry which echoed in Clara's ears was from the other girl's throat, but it could as easily have been from her own. The man was embracing the girl around the waist and lifting her hips, and while his bruising organ slipped in and out of her body, Conrad's finger was slipping in and out of Clara's cunt in the same manner.

But now it was no finger that Clara felt stirring and pounding deep within her. It was a prick, swelling with lust and pride in its own strength. It stretched and filled her furiously as she remembered Conrad's prick to have filled her.

"You're fucking me, darling," she whispered softly

to him. "You shouldn't be fucking me here." She put both arms around his body, licking his lips with her hot little tongue, and as she forced her buttocks against him she twisted them lasciviously from side to side. She drew her mouth away from his wetly. "Please stop fucking me here," she whispered once more. "We can go back to my room if you want me so much now, darling." Her mind told her that she was babbling foolishly, but she whispered again, "Please don't let anyone see you fucking me like this, darling." It seemed to her that her voice must have echoed right across the room, and she blushed scarlet with dismay.

She buried her face in Conrad's coat sleeve, enjoying the rough caress of the material. He plucked his hand slowly from her crotch, and she moaned softly for the loss when he slipped his finger out of her. He raised her face and she saw the finger before her, the one that had been in her cunt. It was glistening wet, and the heavy sweet perfume of her sex clung to it. He brought it closer to her face, and the odor filled her throat as well as her nostrils. It smelled queer, she thought. Did men really like it, she wondered?

"Close your eyes and do exactly as I say," Conrad said softly. Clara obeyed, and then he said, "Put out your tongue!"

She slipped the red tip of her tongue out between her lips, and held her breath to see what would come next. She felt the wet fingertip rub across her tongue, and the sweetish taste of her own sex surprised her. The taste was much better than the smell, she decided.

If she ever did that . . . she did not admit what . . . to Mrs. Burton or any other girl, she would remember to find out if the smell or the taste were nicer. Suddenly the D.A. pressed the tip of his finger against and between her lips. Sticky with her sex, it slid easily into her mouth, startling Clara so much that she closed her teeth sharply on it.

"It isn't to eat," the D.A. reproved her. "It's to be sucked like a candy . . . or a prick." He moved his finger inside her mouth and whispered "Suck it, Clara."

Clara squeezed the finger against the roof of her own mouth and began to suck it. Suddenly she giggled. "It's so very funny," she told him, "to be sucking a thing like a . . . prick . . . and then finding it tastes like a woman." She giggled again.

She turned away from Conrad to the scene across the room. The man was again kneeling behind the girl, and pushing his prick between her buttocks. The girl lowered her head, shaking her hair into wild confusion as the cock thrust into the groove once more. While Clara watched and pondered, Conrad slipped his hand beneath her bottom and began to tickle her tender backside. He duplicated every move that the man made on the girl upon Clara's shrinking body. He rubbed his finger very gently across the yielding aperture, and then he began probing with the tip.

"Push against my finger without resisting," Conrad told her, "then it will slip in easily." And he scratched with his forefinger at the little brown aperture which so temptingly resisted his overtures.

"But it will hurt me," Clara whimpered, staring at what was so clearly happening to the other girl's behind. "Please don't do it to me that way. It hurt ever so much last time!"

"Does she look as if it were hurting her?" the D.A. inquired. He probed a little further between Clara's buttocks as he spoke.

"It's too big!" Clara whispered. "Too big and hairy! Ohhh! It's too big! She mustn't let him do it!"

"It's just because it's big that she likes it," the D.A. replied. "It won't hurt you really. Just tell yourself that you want it, and open yourself up and press down."

Clara rocked her body nervously and tried to give her secret opening to him. His finger pressed harder and was almost into her, and she was suddenly frightened. But the girl on the floor was stirring Clara with her own excitement, and her own resistance weakened.

"If it won't hurt me I'll let you do it," Clara told him without taking her eyes off the couple on the floor. The man was almost up her now. Suddenly the girl uttered a quick gasp and flung her arms wildly from side to side. The prick was penetrating her, deeper and deeper, and she clutched at the rug in a frenzy, while she arched her back and thrust down backwards furiously so as to force the whole cock inside her body. Clara felt as though she had been stabbed. The D.A.'s finger was right inside her now, and was thrusting to and fro as if it would never cease. She began to sob from sheer nervous excitement.

"It hurts!" she exclaimed softly. "It hurts . . . it's so nice. It's so big . . . so big and hairy!"

Conrad twisted his hand about so that his thumb was in Clara's cunt at the same time. Overcome by the bowling hold he was using Clara closed her eyes, and came . . . and came again. And when she opened her eyes once more it was because Conrad was taking his hand out from her crotch.

"You don't have to stop if you don't want to. I rather like it as a matter of fact!" she said. And her hips seemed to lift themselves involuntarily, as if seeking his errant fingers.

He laughed, with a slight edge to it, and Clara felt ashamed. "I don't want to stop, but I must," he said. "There's some business that I must attend to."

He patted her cheek and left. Clara leaned back against the cushions and allowed herself to dream. And then discovered with a start that there was a man standing beside her and looking down at her intently. She peeked at him and decided that she liked his looks. He moved some pillows so as to sit beside her, and accidentally uncovered Clara's panties where she had buried them. He held them up and inspected them critically and Clara reached out her hand and snatched them away.

"They . . . I . . . I was with . . . someone," she stammered, and then realized that it was not quite the right thing to say.

"So I see," the man replied, and she thought with a flurry of shame that he would certainly be able to detect the evidences of her misbehavior with Conrad. She drew her thighs together, but that was of little help to her modesty, for her sex odor was on her fingers and on her mouth too.

With no preamble the man took Clara in his arms. He was kissing her on the mouth, but he was doing more than kissing her, for his hands were running over her whole body, touching her breasts and her thighs and her hips. And Clara did not resist him. She felt a sort of wanton urge toward this sudden familiarity, as though the simple fact of his maleness and her femininity were sufficient excuse. And yet she loved another man. How could she be doing this?

But she was! She kissed the man back hotly. She pressed her breasts against him, and rubbed her thighs across his. She slid her hands around his broad, male shoulders, and knowing that they were watched she nevertheless let the man press her down into the piled up pillows. She stretched out at full length as the man bent above her. He pushed his hand under her dress and raised it. Gently he stroked her bare thighs, and then he slid his hand between Clara's knees, pushing them wide apart.

"Now lift your dress," he whispered, "I want you to show yourself to me."

"Oh! No! The others . . . they . . ." Clara protested feebly.

"They won't care. Not if you're pretty. And besides, they won't see you. I'm the only one who will see you, unless you want them to see you too."

Clara, after a long pause, pulled up her dress a few inches, showing more of her bare legs. "Like that?" she asked him bashfully.

"That's not far enough," she was told. "Lift it higher than that."

She trembled against the man, feeling the sudden throb of his prick against her hip where it touched him. Her cunt was aching with desire. She pulled her skirt up all the way, and clutched it tightly against her stomach while the man saw all her nakedness. "Like that?" she asked softly.

But he did not answer. He made her part her thighs while he ran his hands up and down between them and fingered her cunt. He tickled it and put her hands on his trouser buttons, making her undo them and reach in to take out his prick and fondle it. She wondered why she was so weak and unresisting when she loved another man? Maybe all men were about alike if you were really hot, she thought. But she had been so sure you had to love a man to be excited by him.

Why had she been so sure, she pondered. It wasn't that way with her after all. And while she mused she pressed and squeezed his prick with one hand, and reached in to pull out his balls with the other, cuddling them gently in her palm.

"Perhaps we'd better go in an alcove?" the man was just suggesting, as he drew his trousers together and helped her up with his free arm. And then they were in the alcove, which had one low and very deep chair. She saw herself standing there with her arms crossed over her breasts and squeezing them.

"What do you want me to do?" someone strange was saying in her own voice.

"Strip!" said the man. "Get out of your clothes as quick as you can. Let me see you naked." So Clara undressed in a flurry of garments, letting her clothing drop in a little heap at her feet, until she stood there before him in lovely naked splendor. Feeling the force of his desire beating upon her she turned slowly around in the dim light, allowing the man to feast his eyes on the beauty of her bare body.

"Put your shoes on again," he said after a long pause. "Just your shoes, nothing else." She kicked her feet into her suede shoes and came to him, rubbing her naked body against him like a cat. He told her to put her arms around him and to press her bare body close. He made her squeeze her spread and yielding thighs against his hips and rub her hairy mount on his crotch. Then she had to turn, and with her buttocks pressed down on his thighs she wiggled her hips while he caressed her breasts and flanks and cunt.

"Now go to that chair and kneel down in front of it," he ordered her, to her complete astonishment. But she obeyed him in silence. "And now show me what you would do if there was a man sitting there before you?" he demanded. "Lean toward it and show me."

A fearful shame swept through Clara. She seemed to be kneeling on hot coals, while tongues of flame licked at her naked body and singed the hair of her sex. They laved all her buttocks with burning kisses, darted stinging tongues between her thighs and deep into her slit. And the man was whispering to her again: "If I were sitting there . . . if any man were sitting there . . . what would you do?"

At this moment Clara's imagination was willing to accept any suggestion. She almost believed that there was a man sitting in the chair. She moved forward and inward and her hands reached out to the place where the man's knees would have been. They slid up as if they were resting on the man's thighs, until they met. Lost in her fantasy of pretense her fingers fumbled at imaginary buttons, opened a fly that was not there, and performed the ritual of seeking beneath the underwear and lifting forth a swelling but still soft penis.

Clara stroked and caressed it into full erection, and ran her fingers through the curls that her mind pictured as half-concealing it. Then, lowering her head, she put her soft mouth close to her cupped hands and began to lick and suck a ghostly sex. She forgot her surroundings in a whirl of mental excitement, until she felt a touch on her arm and the man himself slipped into the chair before her.

Clara resisted him when he took her wrists and placed her hands on his thighs. "But I don't even know you," she pleaded.

"That should make it twice as interesting for both of us," he responded. He held her hands there until she became acquiescent, then he leaned back in the chair and thrust his hips forward. "You showed me what you'd do," he reminded her. "Now do it!"

A perverse desire to do what he told her for no other reason than that he was a man once more came over Clara. She could not quite explain it, but equally she could not resist it either. So she clung to his thighs, and then slid her hands along them and upwards. The buttons of his trousers were open. She slipped her feverish fingers in and around his prick, and it pulsed as it lay in her hot palm, growing bigger and bigger as her warm caress incited it.

Suddenly, without even looking at the swelling organ, she leaned forward and closed her lips over the red tip, so that it entered her mouth as far as the ridge. She moved her lips up and down it, wondering that the gesture was already so familiar.

"No! No!" the man was saying, "you must lick it first, you should know how to do that beautifully." And he made her take it out and look at it first, and then put it to her mouth again. She put the tip of her tongue against its tip, and ran it around and around. Then she took it in both hands so as to caress it with her whole tongue, and a fold of the skin slid forward as she did so and closed over the tip of her tongue.

Clara had never come across a foreskin before, but she raised it with the tip of her tongue and licked around it till she reached the ridge at the back. Then she turned her head to one side and ran her wet lips up and down the shaft, nipping with them at the swelling head as it passed to and fro.

She realized that she was reveling in the shame she felt, and her feelings urged her on to further excesses. She held the erect prick in her two hands, kissing it from base to tip, and pressing the bud hard against her lips. She kissed off the juice which was welling out from it, and again prepared to take it into her mouth. But just as she was about to suck it the man pulled away.

"Please," she whispered. The word had slipped out of nowhere and she remembered the girl in the theater yesterday. But she repeated the demand again. "Please . . ." She brought her lips as close to the throbbing cock as the man would permit, and murmured meekly: "Oh! Please let me have it to suck . . ."

When it was in her mouth at last it seemed so enormous that she thought she would choke. She put her hands on his body to push him away, but she could not because he was holding her by the hair. Her hands remained on his stomach in a searching caress, feeling how his sex-hair reached up to his navel in a heavy mat. She tangled her fingers in the hairy thicket while she frantically sucked him off. Tossing her head wildly from side to side, she drew down on his sex with all her might just as her mouth filled with a flood of hot sperm.

Now it was all over . . . and she could realize what had happened. Mute and scarlet with confusion she stumbled to her feet and snatched up her scattered clothing. Huddling them on anyhow, she managed to stagger up the stairs to her room, where she threw herself face down on the bed and burst into a flood of bitter tears.

Chapter 14

The sun was shining brightly when Clara woke the next morning, and for the first few moments she felt deliciously happy and quite a bit refreshed. She stretched and yawned under the warm covers as contented as a kitten, and when the memory of the night before returned to her, she was so shocked that she sat bolt upright.

"It must have been a dream," she told herself. "In a moment I'll remember that it was only a dream." And then her memories stung even more deeply into her realization.

"It was all Conrad's fault," she exclaimed, "He got me all drugged and then left me there." She hurried into the bathroom and plunged under a stinging shower. She slapped on some make-up and hurried down the hall to the D.A.'s bedroom. But there was no one in the room. His breakfast tray showed that his day's program was already under way. Where could he be, she wondered, as she went downstairs and out onto the lawn.

"So here you are!" said a voice behind her, and she spun on her heel to find Mrs. Burton and Bess Lynd and a strange young man carrying a picnic basket standing there and laughing at her. "We were looking for you to go down to the lake and bathe with us and share our picnic," said Alice, passing an arm around her waist.

"And this is my fiancé, Dick! You'll like him . . . when you get to know him!" said Bess, with a naughty smile.

"I'd love to go with you," said Clara, "but wouldn't I be . . . sort of extra?" This last was addressed to Bess.

"You mean don't I want to be alone with him?" asked Bess. "To tell you the truth, I'm afraid to go by myself. He says he hasn't been near a woman for three days, and by now I guess he's just a rapist. I may need you both along quite badly if there's an emergency."

She pinched Clara softly on the behind, with a mocking smile. And they went along through the woods toward the lake, Clara with Bess, and Alice Burton and the man a little ahead. "What do you think of my boy friend?" asked Bess. "I call him Big Dick, but he doesn't like it much. He says it isn't true."

"But why did you ask me along today?" said Clara. "You know I had the idea you didn't like me much. Some of the things you said when I was . . . when we . . . I mean . . ."

"You mean because I said I'd make you beg for it?" said Bess nonchalantly "Don't be silly. That was all part of making love to you, and I don't make love with people I don't like."

"But how can you tell?" Clara objected. "People are so very casual about it here, why you hardly even know the person sometimes. Almost like it was with us."

"When it's casual it's easier to judge people," the

girl contradicted sagely. She was silent for a moment, and then she called out . . . a shade too brightly . . . "What are you two talking about in whispers up there?"

"I was just making Alice an indecent proposition!" called the man over his shoulder. "And what's more, she's accepted it without argument."

"I think you'd better talk to Clara for a while," said Bess very firmly. She walked on ahead to join Alice and Dick dropped back to talk to Clara. "Bess has told me quite a lot about you," he said as he offered her a cigarette. "And what do you think she told me?" At this moment they sighted the lake and Clara was spared the embarrassment of attempting to reply to his query.

"Wonderful for swimming if you have the nerve," said Bess as she sat down and kicked off her shoes and began to peel down her stockings. "Put the beer in the water to cool, you Big Dick you!" she told the man, as she pulled her sweater off over her head.

Alice Burton was already sitting on a flat rock with her shoes off, her dress raised high and showing the lovely line of her bare legs. "Why don't you take your clothes off and have a sun bath?" she asked Clara. "I'm going to, right now."

"But supposing someone came along?" objected Clara. "Three women undressed, alone with one man."

"No one will come by," said Alice. "This is a private estate all along the lake." She leaned toward Clara and then whispered softly in her ear, "Would you like to take off my . . ." She raised her knee and Clara could see up her thigh into the shadow of her crotch.

"They . . . the others are watching," Clara stammered, as she moved away and plucked a flower nervously. She sat down herself and stretched. Then she took off her own shoes and stockings. After a minute she looked around to see what everyone else was doing. Dick had taken off his shirt and was fixing a stone fireplace on the sandy beach. Bess Lynd's sweater was off and her lovely breasts showed nakedly over the tight waist of her skirt. Clara felt her own nipples tighten under her thin dress, and she looked away quickly from Bess's soft pouting pink nipples.

Alice Burton was naked now, and was rolling her hair up in a scarf as she lay back on the grass. She twisted contentedly back and forth and the grass made green stains on her rounded white buttocks. "Why don't you try it?" she called out to Clara. "It feels wonderful to be so free."

"I'm all right," Clara replied uncertainly. She looked again at Bess, who had stripped down to her panties now. They were the briefest ones Clara had ever seen, and hid simply nothing at all. "But you'll want to go in swimming?" said Alice in surprise. "The water's too cold for me," replied Clara.

"Oh! Nonsense, you're too modest, that's all!" said Bess, laughing at her. By this time Dick had completed his job on the fireplace, and having dusted off his hands he unbuckled his belt and with no hesitation at all unzipped his pants and took them off. Then, while Clara tried not to look at him, he walked past her, stark naked, to fetch the picnic basket.

"You have such a wonderful prick, darling," said Bess as he went past her. She reached out to touch it, and then she sat up and kissed it. Clara felt she ought to blush, but no blush came. She turned her head away as a surge of excitement flooded up inside her and her head began to reel.

"Come here, Clara," said Mrs. Burton softly. So Clara turned away from the water and sat down beside her. "Tell me why you are being so foolish about taking off your clothes? Surely you aren't afraid of being seen naked by a man, are you?"

"It isn't that," Clara replied in a burst of honesty. "But it is so evident just how this swimming party is going to end up, and I don't think I want to be part of it . . . not out here in the open in the sunshine with the clouds going by overhead and everything."

Alice didn't say anything as the words tumbled out. She very lazily tickled Clara's bare ankle and leg. Self-conscious, Clara pulled her skirt down to her knees. "You're looking up my skirt!" she whispered, protestingly.

"I wouldn't have to if you took your skirt off," the older woman replied. She drew Clara down beside her. "You're being much more conspicuous by keeping your clothes on," she continued. "Why won't you take them off and let me look at you? It's been a long time since I've seen you naked." And she put her hand under Clara's skirt and fondled her thigh. Upward her fingers ventured and she caressed Clara in the warm and exciting way that had so moved her the first time they had been together.

"And it doesn't matter how this party ends," continued Alice, "no one is going to make you do anything you don't want to do." She touched Clara's fluffy triangle of hair, finally pushing her slim fingers through the curls to the yielding slit and caressing it gently. Clara moved restlessly, and Alice raised her eyebrows at her. "You're tender there today, what have you been doing?" Her words were a soft accusation. "Were you fucked a lot last night?" she added.

Clara tried to brazen the matter out, but it was too much for her. She could not keep her eyes steady, nor restrain a slight trembling of her hands, though she was sure she was not going to blush, and didn't. "I think you have a confession to make to me?" said Alice very softly. She unfastened Clara's skirt and slipped it down her slender legs.

"No! Oh, no! Please!" protested Clara. But her words were disregarded, as the older woman took off her skirt and then her panties. Clara looked apprehensively around to see if Bess and Dick were watching, but they were down in the lake playing boisterously.

"I like that effect when you are left half naked!" said Alice, as she put her head to one side and admired Clara. "When you have the top half on and your slit and everything is all naked . . . very nice indeed." She suddenly rolled Clara over on the grass, squeezing one of her breasts through the thin dress. Her knee pressed down between Clara's legs until they parted, and she rolled in between them and began rubbing her slit up against the girl's. Even while protests were bubbling to Clara's lips she was noticing how soft Alice's sex hair was against her own. "What did you do last night that's made you so tender?" Alice insisted softly, "I think you must have taken on more

209.

than one man, is that it?' She watched Clara curiously, waiting for a tell-tale blush.

"It wasn't anything like that!" Clara cried. "Oh! I can't tell you what it was. Please don't ask me." But Alice did ask, and persisted in it as she rubbed her slit to and fro on poor unresisting Clara, until finally all resistance went out of her. "It was another girl," she admitted finally. "The girl we saw in the theater with the two men. She had a rubber prong and she put it on with a strap round her hips, and she . . . fucked me . . . with it."

"Well, that's not so much," replied Alice judicially, "but if you feel it was wicked, well . . . then you ought to be punished for it. I'll get the other two to help me." Quivering with shame at her words, Clara closed her eyes, and when she opened them again both Bess and Dick were standing beside her, watching Mrs. Burton's hands in between her parted thighs.

"She's been a bad girl and I'm punishing her," stated Alice. "Tell them why I'm punishing you, Clara!" And poor Clara had to relate the story all over again, while Dick got more and more excited as he listened, and his cock began to rise up and quiver. Bess glanced at her fiancé's erection and reached out to pull the foreskin all the way back behind the knob. "Does it excite you, darling?" she laughed mockingly.

"My God!" he exclaimed. "How can you help being excited at a thing like that? I just have to take her now."

Clara rolled over and pressed her thighs together very hurriedly. "Please don't do anything more to me," she begged, "I'm so sore already." She turned her head imploringly to Alice Burton, who bent down to whisper, "I've always wanted to see you fucked, darling."

The man pushed Clara's thighs apart and got in between them. Clara twisted her naked body away from his and tried to escape, but Bess and Alice seized her arms and held her down. "I'll help you to get in, darling," Bess said to the man, and she laughed. "It's funny to think of assisting your future husband in a near rape."

Dick put his hands under the small of Clara's back and lifted her body, rubbing his torso against hers. His hands slid over her buttocks as he pulled her closer. His cock touched her slit and Bess took it in her fingers and rubbed it up and down. He began to thrust the tip harder and harder against her, and she cried out and pleaded with them, but no one listened to her. The two women held her arms tightly, and the man's weight held her to the ground. "Please don't hold my arms like that," begged Clara, feeling that she was going a little crazy.

"Promise not to try and get away?" Bess insisted. "Will you promise to lie still and let Dick fuck you if we let you go?" And Clara nodded her head. "I promise!" she whispered.

"Then put your arms around him," Bess ordered, and Clara shut her eyes and embraced her stallion. He began thrusting down at her in sensual fury. "Fuck back at him!" insisted Bess. "Raise your behind and wiggle! You'll like it if you help!"

She was right, too. Clara felt the pain of his entry and the soreness of her over-worked slit disappear, and excitement began to pour through her limbs and stimulate her senses. "Ohh! Ohh!" she cried. "Fuck me! Please fuck me, darling! I can't wait for it!" She felt her own crisis imminent, and suddenly the man cried out "Bess!" and pulled out his cock. The girl was already on her knees beside him with her waiting mouth, and she hugged his hips as he spurted his hot flood down her throat.

He rolled over on his side while Bess was sucking at his cock, and Clara was left with a terrible aching empty sort of feeling in her cunt. It gaped widely and seemed to be almost sucking in the empty air, begging mutely for the man to come back.

Bess Lynd bent over Clara and said, "He'll have another hard-on in a few minutes if I kiss him some more. Shall I ask him to fuck you again? He will if I ask him to." And Clara gave a frantic nod of assent.

"But you have to do something for me," the girl added. "Do you remember something that I wanted you to do to me before and that you refused? I told you then that some day you'd beg me on your knees to let you lick my behind?"

"Oh! No! Not that! Not while they're here!" pleaded poor Clara, as she drew the girl's face down to hers and whispered, "I'll do it as soon as we get back to the house. We can go to my room, and I'll do it to you there. But please, please tell him to fuck me again now?"

"No!" said Bess, with a determined shake of her head, "I said you'd go down and beg me, and you will too, while they are here."

Suddenly Clara twisted herself to her knees in front

of Bess Lynd. She turned her face upward and pleaded: "Please let me lick your ass?" and she moved forward on her knees as Bess retreated. She put her face down to kiss the girl's naked thighs, following her imploringly.

By this time she was begging her heatedly. "Let me do it, let me lick your behind! They can watch if they want to, I don't care." And finally Bess seemed satisfied and sat down on the grass and told Clara to lie with her head between her soft thighs. And Clara kissed her slit and her buttocks, and then put her mouth to the girl's little ass-hole as she lifted her legs high in the air. She kissed it first, and then she put her tongue tip to it. It felt moist and puckered and something like a tiny cunt, but Clara's heart seemed to stop, so overcome with shame she felt. Her tongue was caressing the girl's anus very softly, passing back and forth, and she was smothered in the soft curly hair between the girl's buttocks.

"Dick!" Bess suddenly cried out, "fuck me now, while she is doing this!" Clara wanted to cry out that she was being cheated, but the man was suddenly above them both, his red cock only an inch or two from Clara's mouth. She had to keep on with her licking of Bess's behind while the swelling weapon drove on down into the slit, and then Dick's balls were brushing across Clara's face at every thrust he gave. And then, quite by chance, Clara's tongue slipped up and touched his hot cock. She jerked her head away with an abrupt sob, but the girl was much too occupied to notice it.

Clara turned in despair to Mrs. Burton. "Would you like me to lick your ass too? Would you?" Alice smiled softly at her and replied "Why, yes, Clara, if you want to." So Clara buried her face under Alice's buttocks and put her mouth to this other anus. She licked it and sucked it and poked her tongue at it, and then Alice said, "I think you ought to take a dip in the lake now!"

"But I want to get fucked," Clara protested, "that's why I . . . why I . . ." and she stopped.

"Let's all take a dip," cried Bess, as she thrust Dick away from her and jumped to her feet. And in a minute they were all in the water, splashing and shouting. The lake was cold and made them feel very much alive, and presently Bess whispered to Clara, "You do like Dick, don't you?"

"Oh! Bess!" Clara whispered back, "you are going to let him finish fucking me, aren't you?"

"Of course I am, silly," said Bess, splashing water all over her. "He's going to fuck the lot of us. What do you think he's here for?" And she planted a wet kiss on the end of Clara's nose as she continued. "We had it all arranged before we left the house this morning." And she looked at Clara teasingly and added, "You really do need it, don't you? And after what you did last night, too! I'm surprised at you." Clara felt she would never stop blushing.

Clara didn't know if she understood such freedom and lack of jealousy. In fact she wasn't sure of anything at the moment, except that she wanted a man inside her. Women's passions are more tenacious than men's, very few of whom would have stayed hot after a dip in that cold water. But when a woman makes up her mind to be laid at a certain time, she gets hot at that time and stays hot till something is done about it.

But at the moment the others wanted their picnic, and Clara had to sit and eat and drink with the rest of them, and burn up inside all the time, until at last Dick leaned back with a yawn of repletion and said bluntly: "I feel quite like fucking. Who wants to be laid?"

"I do!" cried his fiancée, and Alice Burton seconded her. Clara put in her claim, and the three of them chorused at him like schoolgirls until he shook his head disapprovingly. "You remind me of a nest of baby robins waiting with their mouths wide open to get a worm," he mocked.

"I love worms!" Bess declared. "Especially long wiggly ones like this!" And she struck his soft prick with her slim fingers from underneath and bounced it up in the air. Then she added, "But as we can't all be first, why don't we all lie down in a row and show you what we've got to offer and let you choose?"

That seemed a brilliant idea, a sort of modern version of the judgment of Paris from the Greek mythology, and the three women were soon stretched out on the grass side by side, offering a lovely display of feminine nudity. Dick walked to and fro, regarding them critically, while they parted their legs invitingly or amorously jiggled their breasts at him. He stroked his chin in deep thought. "Turn over!" he commanded, and the three rolled over and displayed a row of lovely plump buttocks for his inspection.

"It can't be decided this way," he said at last. "The best way would be to go back to the house and get

215

help, but that would take too long, and anyway I don't want to share you with any other man."

"Well, which of us distressed females did you fuck last of all?" asked Bess Lynd.

"Alice," he replied quite candidly. Without pausing he added, "We had a quick one in the water before lunch, and we damn near got drowned. But you know I never did finish Clara off properly! You remember you grabbed me away at the last moment?" he added, turning to Bess Lynd.

"Then Clara comes first, and Alice is last, and I'm in the middle," Bess decided. She turned to Clara, "He's all your property, honey, but there's something I've got to attend to first." She plunged at her man as she spoke, and took his shrunken prick in her wet little mouth. Under her lascivious tonguing he was soon standard size again, and she pushed him toward Clara.

The cold water had evidently had an astringent effect on her slit, for it was so tight that it hurt her as Dick's cock slipped in. The aroused pulse of her blood had made her skin very sensitive too, and she was terribly excited by the touch of his curly hair as it rubbed between her legs and over her slit. She writhed and twisted her stomach roughly against him, and made him take her pert breasts in his hands and tease her hard little nipples. Her whole body was thrilling in quick response to his fierce thrusts.

She wriggled her buttocks indecently in her efforts to excite him further, helping him to plunge his cock deeply into her womb, holding her thighs up and apart with her hands and pressing down with her muscles to cause her slit to open as far as possible. A little voice whispered that what she was doing was very naughty, and she told the little voice to take a flying fuck at itself. The hot prick was stretching her so unbearably, thrusting deep between her moist and swelling sex lips, and her body delighted in what her conscience protested.

Clara felt fingers slipping along her body and up to her hard little nipples. Feminine fingers, touching her with feminine lightness and feminine desire. Alice Burton squeezed her breasts and tickled her nipples, and then she slid her head in between the man and his girlish mount and began to suck the aching nipples.

Bess began touching Clara too, caressing the soft lines of her thighs and running her fingers under the writhing buttocks, to hook one forefinger into her asshole and twist it around inside. Clara began to choke with a nervous sobbing as her body succumbed to the onslaught of three pairs of hands and a hotly possessive prick.

Dick locked his body against hers, and Clara could feel the deep hard stab of his prick within her. Then came the thrilling feel of the hot flood as he spent, and she thought that the warm jets were splashing up inside her womb itself, as his fingers clenched in esctasy deeply into the soft flesh of her tender loins. She tore her own nails deep into the grass beneath her, and drummed her little heels against the small of his back, throwing her head from side to side in ecstasy.

And all the time Alice kept kissing her on the mouth, twining her tongue against hers, while at the same moment Bess was prodding her forefinger up that tender ass-hole. If she went any higher she would faint, Clara felt certain, and then her crisis caught her and she screamed aloud in hysterical happiness.

Bess Lynd had been so excited watching Clara come that when she opened her eyes as Dick pulled gently out of her she threw her arms around her fiancé and gasped, "I don't want you to fuck me yet, I'd sooner suck you off."

She took him into her wet little mouth and stretched out on her belly with her head in his lap. Her lips sucked and kissed and her hot little tongue teased at the rejuvenated cock. "Show them how soon you come when I do this, darling!" she whispered, squeezing his balls and rubbing her fingers hard against the spot between his balls and his anus.

"Or show us how quickly I can make you come, Bess," said Alice Burton, slipping her body between the girl's knees and placing nibbling kisses on the soft insides of her thighs.

"Please," Clara whispered, so softly that she could hardly hear herself. "Please don't. Don't let me see you lick any other woman . . ."

But Alice heard nothing of this. She put her hot lips on Bess Lynd's open cunt and pushed them between the melting sex-lips, kissing and sucking. The end of her tongue appeared and began to run up and down in the deep red slit. She kissed the girl's buttocks and lips and then she thrust her tongue into the gaping cunt and fucked in and out with it. Clara saw the group of three grow more and more excited. Alice clutched one of Bess's legs between hers and began to toss herself off against the soft thigh, while she held the girl's slit open with her hand in order to squeeze her mouth further into it.

At this moment Dick could hold back no longer, and Clara could see the pulsing of his prick as he shot down into Bess's eager throat. As she swallowed the hot sperm she seemed to become even more passionate, and as soon as she had sucked him dry she turned to Alice and clutched her head fiercely in both hands. Crouching above her she rubbed her slit in keen delight over the other woman's face and mouth, fucking as passionately as if the tongue within her were a real prick piercing her yielding slit. Her sensuality had grown to such a pitch that her love juice was dripping down and spreading all over Alice's lips and face.

Clara covered her face with her hands. "I don't want to see it!" she cried softly. "I don't want her to do it to anyone but me!" The writhing pair rolled over on the grass and lay there panting and quiescent.

"I had to do it to her, Clara," Alice Burton told her after a while, still lying with her head between Bess Lynd's parted legs. "Can't you see that she made me do it to her, just as I made you do it to me?"

"Please come away from her," Clara begged. She tugged at Bess Lynd's leg and said, "I'll do it to you instead, if you will stop making Alice do it. I'll lick your cunt myself!" She did not know why the sight of Alice doing this had agitated her so terribly, but there was nothing that she would not do to prevent it happening again.

"Oh! Clara, you silly girl," said Alice. "You should know I like to be made to do it. You ought to know how very exciting it is to be made to suck off a ̇ice lovable cunt!" She put her arms around the girl's legs once more, amorously embracing them and making sure that Clara was watching, and then pressed kiss after kiss on the moisture laden lips of her eager slit.

"Don't talk any more about doing it!" exclaimed Bess Lynd. "Lick it instead!" She thrust her hips down on Alice's face with firm decision, and in a moment she was spending once more, while Clara turned her head away in dismay. Young girls are funny. Clara felt terribly ashamed, as she watched Alice wiping her cheeks across the other girl's thighs, and reaching immediately afterwards for the man's prick. She glanced with a smile at Clara, a smile of lascivious amusement, and then she whispered something in the man's ear.

Dick got into position behind her, kneeling between her legs, as she lifted her bottom high in the air and laid her breasts and face on the grass, glancing at Clara to make sure she was looking. He put his cock between the elevated buttocks, rubbing the tip on her little pink ass-hole.

"Don't do that!" cried Clara. "I'll watch him fuck you if you want me to, but don't let him do that. I can't bear it!"

"Why ever not?" queried Alice. "This is fucking too. And besides, you made me want it this way, sucking my ass with your frisky little tongue."

Clara saw the rampant prick probe into the deep crease between the rounded buttocks, and then begin to disappear in the tight little hole. She gasped as if it were happening to her.

Alice twisted her body about as though she were being tortured, but an expression of ecstatic pleasure came to her face. "Oh! Clara darling!" she exclaimed suddenly, "you'll never know how big a prick can feel till you've had one up your ass." As a matter of fact Clara knew quite a bit about it, but she wouldn't admit it, and anyway to see it being done to Alice made her furiously jealous.

"Shall I tell you what it's like?" Alice asked her with a smile. "Shall I tell you how hairy it feels and how it seems to stretch you open unendurably, and how it presses inside and how deep down you feel the end? If it goes in any further it will come out in my throat!" she exclaimed.

"Then I'll suck the end of it and make him spend!" said Bess Lynd maliciously.

Clara stopped her ears with her hands, but she could still hear Alice's voice. Some women are like that, they like to keep on talking about what they're doing in bed, even while they're doing it. "First you think it hurts," Alice was saying, "and then you decide that it doesn't. It's just stretching you almost to death, and it's simply wonderful. But sometimes it drives you just insane . . . and then . . . Oh! Clara! Clara! He's spending. I can feel it. And I can't . . . I can't . . . I . . ." She was coming too, and Clara didn't want to see it happen, and she jumped up and stumbled away into the shadow of the trees.

She felt very little-girlish and forlorn and kind of sorry for herself as she walked away around some rocks out of sight. She was coming out into a little clearing

221

around a sort of cabin, when she heard footsteps behind her. She suddenly realized that she was still naked, and she jumped off the path and behind a tree.

A man was coming along the path toward the cabin with a small leather case in his hand. She peeked out at him and then ducked back in dismay. It was Conrad. She would have just called out to him if he had been alone. But behind him she could see there was a girl.

She shrank further back into the trees, and by the time her curiosity had stimulated her courage to decisive action they had passed by and she could only see their rear view. The girl had a nice figure, she thought, and she was clad in a tan skirt and a white sweater and was wearing high-heeled shoes. For some reason Clara thought she was vaguely familiar, and then she decided not, adding in her own mind that it was not a practical outfit to be using out in the woods. And then she remembered her own scanty outfit once more, and found that she was blushing furiously.

Curiosity made her decide to stay where she was a little longer and see what happened. She meditated about the curious situation, deciding that although she might have thought early in the day that she hated Conrad very much indeed, she was now bitterly jealous of the girl instead. "He didn't wait long to find someone else," she told herself, as she tiptoed nearer to the cabin and looked and listened.

Not a sound came from it so far, and then she smelled smoke and saw a wisp of it coming from the cabin chimney. Then a long time, or what seemed a long time passed, and suddenly a muffled cry came from inside. This really scared her, and she was trying to make up her mind to escape when she heard the back door of the cabin open.

The D.A. and the girl came around the corner, and she stood on tiptoe and kissed him, while he gently patted her buttocks with a caressing gesture. Clara feared for a moment that she would be discovered when they turned down the path. But the D.A. and the girl were both too engrossed in each other to make any outside discoveries.

Clara leaned against a tree and gasped with sudden and overwhelming pain. "Rita! Rita here! Ohh! Rita darling!" she whispered to herself, unbelievingly. But they came walking on down the path, and she realized that it was all too true. Her sister had one hand inside the belt of Conrad's trousers, and she was smiling up at him in the starry-eyed way common to girls in love.

Clara dodged round the trees to avoid them, and as they went on toward the house she ran around to the back door of the cabin and went in. She just had to find out . . . if there was anything to find out. She looked hastily around the room. The fire was dying down. The D.A. had brought a leather case with him, she remembered. Where was it? Quick, before he missed it and came back to get it. In a moment more she had it in her hands, and had raised the lid. Inside it was what she had expected and yet feared to see. She had known in her heart what it would be.

A little steel brand with a delicate silver handle, and it was beautifully carved . . . into the figure of a scorpion!!

Other Titles Available from Blue Moon